Holding Woman

AND OTHER STORIES OF ACCEPTABLE MADNESS

Bilingual Press/Editorial Bilingüe

Publisher
Gary Francisco Keller

Executive Editor
Karen S. Van Hooft

Associate Editors
Brian Ellis Cassity
Amy K. Phillips
Linda K. St. George

Address
Bilingual Press
Hispanic Research Center
Arizona State University
PO Box 875303
Tempe, Arizona 85287-5303
(480) 965-3867

KELLEY JÁCQUEZ

Holding Woman

AND OTHER STORIES OF ACCEPTABLE MADNESS

Bilingual Press/Editorial Bilingüe

TEMPE, ARIZONA

Library of Congress Cataloging-in-Publication Data

Jácquez, Kelley.
  Holding woman and other stories of acceptable madness / Kelley Jácquez.
    p. cm.
  ISBN 978-1-931010-86-3 (pbk. : alk. paper)
1. New Mexico—Social life and customs—Fiction.   I. Title.
  PS3610.A35687H65 2012
  813'.6—dc23
                              2012021298

PRINTED IN THE UNITED STATES OF AMERICA
Front cover art: Holding Redemption *(2012) by Dolores Comstock*
Cover and interior design by John Wincek, Aerocraft Charter Art Service

SYNONYMS

Beyond light is shadow,
And behind the shadow
There is probably no light
And no shade. No sound, no silence.
Call it eternity, or God, or Hell.
But don't call it nothing,
As if nothing had happened.

Francisco Brines
SPANISH POET (1932–)

Contents

Acknowledgments

T his book is dedicated to my mother, Cassandra Dunn Kendall, who loved me more than I ever realized. Courageous against impossible odds, and victorious in all endeavors, thank you for your examples of work ethic, integrity, and fortitude.

For Dr. Robert O'Neil, professor emeritus, California State University, Fresno, who was the first person to say, "Write me a story," and then demanded I do it, although I argued with him that I didn't know how.

For Carolyn Hughes, my dear friend, cara hermosa, who unfailingly read unfinished, nascent, and confusing stories yet continued to urge, "Keep writing." My first psychologist, my first editor, thank you for your valuable time and encouragement.

This book is also dedicated to my two sons, Isaiah and Samuel, who remembered to capture the posters from the bookstore where I gave my first public reading and then hung them on the walls at home saying, "See Mom, you're a real writer. It says so right there."

For JoAnne Carol Bassett, my oldest friend, who kept telling me that I had worth even while we stood next to each other rolling burritos for minimum wage and imagined little more for the future. Dearest JoAnne, thank you for seeing only the good in me, and ignoring the rest. Deepest gratitude for the thousands of belly laughs, Sister-woman. (JoAnne died January 6, 2012 of heart failure and I will miss her throughout the rest of my life.)

For my Mark, my savior, my sweetheart, my dearest darling, the bravest man I've ever known, thank you for your tireless support, enduring love, patience beyond the call of commitment, and your strength.

For my brother Ed DeArman, thank you for thinking I walk on water. As you already know, I love you, Brudder. Thank you for buying me the printer so I could write this book.

For Ofelia Jácquez: Thank you for your myriad examples of what a human being should strive to be: patient, tolerant, kind to all who cross your path, but able to defend your dignity; unmovable in character, belief, and morality. I am humbled before you.

A thousand thanks to Gordy Webster, owner, publisher of the *Business Journal*, Fresno, CA, for the experience and education I received while working with you. Thank you for the challenges and the fourteen-hour days, and for entrusting me with your newspaper(s). I learned so much. Thank you to Reo Carr, my first editor-in-chief, for his stunning examples of "grace under pressure."

To Meryl Soto, Francesca Hampton, and Christine Shaw, all dedicated teachers and profound thinkers, thank you for your invaluable contributions to the world.

Thank you to Linda St. George, editor, for being a dream come true to work with; Gary Keller, Regents' Professor, Hispanic Research Center; Karen Van Hooft, executive editor; and all at Bilingual Press who worked on and believed in this book.

The Joke

In the giggled whispers of altar boys, and women's reminders not to disturb Father Morris after four o'clock in the afternoon, it was rumored that he had taken to drink. Everyone ignored the signs, among them his contemplated speech and exaggerated enunciation when surprised by a parishioner late on a weekday, the falling forward or to the side when observed picking up trash or tending flowers around the church, the forgetfulness and early departures from celebrations.

The men of El Nido especially ignored the old father's telltale cues. Many had their own habits to hide, so the signs were not things they were inclined to point out in others.

Some couldn't imagine that a man might willingly forgo the feel of feminine flesh, and so felt Father Morris had a right to drink.

The women of the church assured themselves that Father nipped only a little, for his health, for the pains that attack an aging body. They agreed it was those very things that had created his indulgence in the first place. They called upon long memories of some twenty-eight years that—while the old man was neither imaginative or enthralling in his sermons—he hummed when performing baptisms or last rites, and his answer to all tragedy was to question less and pray more—he was a good and simple man who set a traditional example of what a priest should be at Our Lady of the Blessed Virgen de Guadalupe in El Nido, New Mexico, population 264.

On a particularly beautiful Sunday in late May, Father Morris ascended to the pulpit with help from his altar boys, two on each side. The old man gripped the lectern with both hands while he attempted to recite the opening liturgy. His words slid into each other, and his body waved about as if struggling to stand straight against the roll of a ship. At last, Father Morris gave up his charade and leaned fully against the pulpit, curling the knots of his knuckles over the front edge, and smiled.

"A flub comes," began Father Morris. The old priest rubbed at the hair above his right temple, sending the white tufts into a miniature snow flurry and shifting his biretta to sit sideways on his head.

"There was a man," he began again. "And a flood comes."

Father Morris swept a robed arm from side to side as if the flood was about to engulf the very room in which his parishioners sat.

"The man climbs to the top of hees house—to escape the flood. He beliefs himself a good Chrisman and a demoted beliefer in the mirmicals of God."

At this point Father Morris began to laugh. He laughed long enough that his parishioners thought he'd lost his place, and the story, however he had decided to tell it, was over.

As if rehearsed, a concurrence of throat clearing and covered coughs echoed throughout the church. The crowd resettled itself, moving from one haunch to the other, uncrossing and recrossing legs, women checking the pins holding up hairdos, men sliding cowboy boots against the wood floor, looking for a relaxed position.

Soon Father Morris resumed his narrative and the story went on to say that although a man in a rowboat and then a helicopter came to offer help, the man refused and answered that he was waiting for God to save him.

To illustrate his despair at the man's refusals of help, Father Morris dropped his head and wagged it from left to right with increasing speed until he felt himself going sideways, then grappled for the lectern to set himself upright again. The biretta's tenuous hold on the priest's scalp gave way with the first wag and landed at the base of a lit candle, sending a thrill of concern and a chorus of stifled gasps throughout the first three rows of the church. Sheriff Maximillan Venezuela, sitting with his wife, Perla, in the front row, farthest left, intermittently shifted his gaze to the candle throughout the rest of Father's presentation.

Hortencia Alcón gave Emily Trujillo a raised eyebrow and a prankish smile as if to say, "I told you so." Emily responded by putting an index finger to her mouth, then covering her smile with a handkerchief.

With religion as the only solace left to her, Maggie Serna refused to absorb what was before her and huddled the youngest of her seven children closer to her breasts.

Still learning the language of her new country and able only to speak in the present tense, Yolanda Móntez concentrated a concerned look into the father's face. She leaned forward to watch his mouth, but the words remained unfamiliar. She was used to the drone of blessings, pleas for mercy, and reminders of God's power and grace presented in Latin. For Yolanda, it had not yet become clear that the priest was telling a joke.

When recognition of Father's condition reached the back pew, Della Mondregal experienced what she felt to be a revelation. It could not be otherwise. What more blessed place, and who more reliable to deliver the message? Della believed she now had her answer and would never have to leave her house again. She was entitled to stay home sipping the same sort of consolation as Father Morris had drunk into his soul that very morning.

"The next thing," continued Father Morris, "water walshes the roof and the man is slept away."

The pause was dramatic—the priest pointing a bent finger toward heaven and his voice cracking with emotion—". . . an' the man's shoul ashends to haven."

From the trailer park where she lived in Aztec, Ruby Rodríguez had driven seventeen miles to El Nido that morning to have coffee with her sister Salina and attend Mass. She believed she should attend Mass more often because she had really bad luck with men and thought perhaps if she prayed more, God might lift the curse. Ruby sat with her sister, resolved that this was the first of many Sundays toward her new lifestyle and a renewed understanding of God. Instead, Ruby turned to Salina for an understanding of Father Morris, which wasn't possible at the moment since Salina had both hands over her mouth, her eyes all asquint with tiny tears squeezed into the eyelashes, her belly heaving as if preparing to throw up, and unable to breathe with uncontrollable laugher.

"God welcomed the man pursonly," said Father Morris, "but the man looked disdressed. So God said to the man, 'What is it, my som?'

"And the man answered, 'I beliefed in you, but you let me drown.'"

At last, believed the audience, it was the culmination, the climatic phrase, the old man's moment to deliver the grand finale.

With the same bluish-white finger pointing to the hereafter, his arm rising above his shoulder, Father Morris cried out in exasperation as he quoted the Almighty. "'I sent you a bloat and a hemoclopter—what more did you want?'"

The entire congregation had heard the joke before, to be sure, and believed they grasped the full meaning of the punch line, but remained confused about how to react.

Although Father Morris wasn't able—considering his condition—to actually see the individual faces of his parishioners, he had expected something more than a repeated round of near silence, shifting in seats, and shushing of children.

The priest blinked several times behind his trifocals, stretched his corrugated neck like a turtle inspecting its environment, then slowly withdrew it back into his stiff collar. He turned away and flapped an arm at the congregation as he descended the steps, nearly falling into the arms of an altar boy, and said, "Look for moats and hellochoppers. They are all around you."

Yolanda didn't understand that this meant Mass was over, so she looked to others for an appropriate reaction.

It was no help.

Much of the congregation simply looked on and accepted the odd Sunday service. These things happen, believed the people of El Nido. They watched the priest stumble to the bottom of the steps, then wave off the assistance of the altar boys once he reached flat ground. Men waited for wives to decide when it was time to rise and file from the church; women reacted with a deep intake of breath that pushed them to their feet and returned them to thoughts of daily duties. There were tortillas to be rolled out and Sunday dinner to be cooked, after all.

Sheriff Max got up and blew out the candle, then took Perla by the hand and they left the church quietly down the side aisle.

Ruby and Salina were doubled over, hanging on to each other, red-faced, tears running down their cheeks.

Della looked relieved, as if disburdened from a duty she would never have to perform again.

Maggie Serna looked terrified, her mind racing, thinking that when she reached the end of her life her priest would be in no condition to absolve the mortal sin fated to come pounding at her door. As it turned out, Father Morris died before Maggie anyway, and, of course, there was indeed a competent priest at Maggie's side to forgive her.

Although Hortencia acknowledged Emily's wagging finger of shame, the smile of insider knowledge remained on her lips as she exited the church.

The following week, Father Morris received only one acknowledgment of his behavior the Sunday before. Sheriff Max arrived at the church on Wednesday, settled himself into the confessional, and repeated the obligatory phrase, "Forgive me, Father, for I have sinned."

Prompted by the priest to commence his confession, Sheriff Max began his account.

"I have a friend," said Max. "A long time we know each other. I stopped him for drunk driving. I took him to jail. . . . I cost him money, ruined his reputation, and caused him shame. . . . He is my friend. I love him. But I could not let him do that. . . . Did I do right, Father?"

The two men sat without speaking. Each of them shifted in his chair. Each took out a handkerchief, and on both sides of the curtain, each man attempted to strangle small noises of anguish and embarrassment.

As was his custom, once Sheriff Max was satisfied that he'd made himself clear, he felt no compulsion to repeat himself, so he waited for Father Morris to end the meeting.

Father Morris knew this and finally spoke aloud. "I will pray for your friend, Maximillan. You did the right thing."

The following Sunday, the regulars—which was most of El Nido, except for Della—returned to church. For most, all was right with their world again. Father Morris appeared in full costume, according to his usual custom, and droned the familiar promises and admonishments.

El Nido, once again, was restored to sanity and sanctuary.

One Night...

I t was the winter of 1974 and the northwest corner of New Mexico had been warned to brace itself for one of the coldest winters on record. The evening news presented colored charts with meteorological comparisons of similar conditions and locked in a forecast. More convincing were the Apache medicine men who had predicted it long before the official report. The holy men knew to watch small animals hoarding food earlier than usual, and hoarding more of it. They watched the hair of horses and sheep grow thicker before the first freeze, and they smelled on the wind the coming suffocation of air too cold to breathe. These things they had watched for centuries, and they were never wrong.

There was no wind this night. The frost came silently, like the cold attacking a beef roast thrown into the freezer, surrounding first the outer layer, then steadily piercing through inches of meat until it reaches bone. Animals make no sounds during such cold, and people sleep closer together, even if the house is warm, as if they know, deep in the unconsciousness of slumber, what lies just on the other side of the wall.

The cold promised to freeze pipes, kill car batteries, and grow frost on the insides of windows. Most folks leave a trickle of water going down the kitchen sink all night to make sure there is running water come morning. This was something the secretary at the El Nido Water Association preyed upon because it meant overcharging customers that month without detection. Most customers simply accepted the bill, muttering, "Well, there

were all those cold nights in December, after all." Nine years of
running water down the drains of El Nido tallied in the tens of
thousands of ghostly dollars when all was said and done—enough
money for the secretary to buy her disappearance into Guaymas,
Sonora, Mexico, after the complaints reached the state capital and
the commission sent investigators. They found the second set of
books lying in plain sight on top of a filing cabinet.

But that's another story, and the scandal concerning the
secretary padding the bills and pocketing the money was years
from unfolding. This night, the water would be left running and
the thought of paying the bill would occur after it arrived in the
mail. This night had nothing to do with the water association
secretary. This night had been set aside for a miracle.

At 6:30 on Saturday night Lily was ready to close the bar by
seven. Her only customers were Hilario Armenta and Adolfo
Flores, and Lily knew she could bribe them into leaving if she
bought a round and appealed to their gentle natures that her feet
hurt and electricity cost money. Driving his rounds, Sheriff Max
stopped to ask if Lily had any troublemakers. She pointed to the
end of the bar where the middle-aged best friends stood talking
in low voices and sipping their beer. Sheriff Max smiled and told
Lily to call if she needed anything.

Just as Lily was about to ask the men to leave, Della Mondregal
slipped through the door and closed it quickly behind her. Why she
chose what was to be one of the coldest nights in El Nido's recorded
history to get tired of drinking alone was anybody's guess. It was
rumored that Della was dying of cancer, although nobody knew
what kind or if she was doing anything about it. They knew only
that she stayed in her home most of the time, had the phone discon-
nected, and quit going to Mass at Our Lady of Guadalupe.

T wenty-five miles west of El Nido on Highway 46 is McGee Park, the closest thing to a concert hall for all of northwest New Mexico. It's where wrestling matches are held, classic cars are displayed, and rodeos enthrall audiences. For the Freddy Fender concert the sawdust and horse manure had been swept away, folding chairs were set out in straight rows, and colored lights hung from the tall ceiling.

Salina Gonzales checked her purse for tickets to the concert and left her husband at home as she always did because he didn't like going anywhere anyway, and drove to the house of Yolanda Móntez. Salina was a woman nearing fifty who accepted life for just what it was, neither railing against it nor speaking in favor of it. Nothing seemed to bring Salina to her knees. Not her taciturn husband—not the daughter who ran away and then called home intermittently to scream garbled obscenities over the phone, then ask for money—and not the son who had been accused of molesting the daughter of the woman he was living with in North Carolina and hanged himself before the trial. At the funeral of her son, Salina shocked those who sat closest trying to comfort her when she said that it was better to be the mother of a son who had committed suicide than the mother of a convicted child molester and she was grateful to her son for making the choice.

When Yolanda got into the car, she asked Salina if she had had any trouble getting away from her husband. Salina answered no, there was no trouble; he simply hid behind his copy of the *Farm News* the way he always did, all sour at the mouth, and grunted when she reached for the handle at the front door. Yolanda laughed and said in her broken English, "Amiga, I had seen you esposo es-smile." Salina told Yolanda not to take his smiles too seriously. "That was probably because he'd just run over something small and helpless with the tractor," said Salina.

Yolanda was a woman in her midthirties with five children and carrying a sixth in her belly. She had no money to spend on a concert to see Freddy Fender, but Salina had convinced her to go after showing her an extra ticket and promising to have her home by eleven o'clock. Yolanda's husband was not consulted about her going to the concert because he would have said no. Instead, Yolanda had given her husband his afternoon meal and his lunch box and waved him out the door more sweetly than usual for the swing shift at the San Juan power plant.

This night, the two women, dressed in the frocks they usually wore to weddings, would become two young girls again while watching un ídolo mexicano who conjured heart flutters like those of the first time they had ever been alone with a boy. Filled with youth, the women giggled as they passed the El Nido Bar, then turned around and pulled into the parking lot, vowing just one drink—a soda for Yolanda—and only one song on the jukebox.

⸺ ◦ ⸺

Della had been sitting at the bar for only a few minutes when Hortencia Alcón hobbled in and used her cane to shut the door. She began to explain to no one in particular that it was too late and too far to drive to the feed store in Bloomfield for teat medicine, so she was coming to get a bottle of cheap, strong whiskey to rub on the cow's udder before treating it with Corona Bag Balm. Della looked at her through half-closed eyes, saying she was impressed as hell with Hortencia's home remedies—and her alibi—and told Lily to bring Hortencia whatever she was drinking. The old woman wasn't prone to drink, and she really had come to the bar in search of relief for her cow and not herself, but she knew Della was dying and felt it would cost her nothing to fill the space next to Della for just a little while.

⸺ ◦ ⸺

After parking her car some ten yards up the dirt road winding behind the bar, Dolores Álvarez leaned against the door of the

El Nido Bar as if fearing to wake someone on the other side. She peeked her head around the rim of the door, the volume of her wiry hair entering like a fur hat at the end of a mop slipping through a doorway to scare children. Finally her whole body came through the door and she scurried to the women at the bar with a fast hello and chose a stool next to Della, where she sat biting at a fingernail and watching the door. No one was quite sure what might happen if her husband Geraldo entered the bar, but whatever it was, the people of El Nido had grown to rely on the Álvarez couple to provide amusing morning-coffee conversation. The townspeople feasted on the details of the latest scrimmage inflamed by infidelity or the contrived and complicated dramas orchestrated to foment displays of affection.

Everyone's favorite story was the time Dolores bought a gun and drove to the Montoya Pick-a-Dent wrecking yard, resolved to murder Geraldo after finding a tube of lipstick—not her color— on the floorboard of the car. Knowing she was about to kill her husband, Dolores cried the whole way to the wrecking yard. It had to be done, though. Cheating was a murdering offense in New Mexico; everybody knew that.

Her face swollen and red, Dolores drove past the wrecking yard office without stopping to check in. As the dust flew behind the '68 Mercury, Freddy Montalvo grabbed his keys, locked up the greasy office, and left for the day. He'd seen that face before on a couple of ex-wives and decided it was best to let love take its natural course without any witnesses or innocent bystanders.

Dolores wound her car along the narrow path leading deeper into the piles of twisted metal until she came to a broad spot in the road and pulled over. She checked her lipstick in the rearview mirror and began loading bullets into the pistol as the man at the pawnshop had shown her. When she finished, she noticed she hadn't removed the price tag hanging from the trigger guard and then was afraid to take it off now that the gun was loaded. She left it where it was, hoping it wouldn't get in the way.

She walked up the road, calling Geraldo's name until he appeared from behind a rusted Plymouth. He smiled at Dolores, dropping his wrench in the dirt as he walked toward her with his hands turned out, but his smile turned to a squint and fell into slackened lips of disbelief as Dolores raised the gun. It looked like a toy with its tiny mechanisms, pea-sized barrel, and stupidly swinging price tag, but Geraldo knew the gun was no toy and Dolores's face told him this was no joke.

Geraldo heard the first pop and then a ricochet as the bullet bounced off a decapitated Ford. The second bullet whizzed past his face and the third spun off into space. Another ended up hitting the dirt at about the same time as Geraldo, his feet tangled in distributor wires and sagebrush. Dolores walked toward him, pointing the gun at his chest. She had to think for a second which side his heart was on, then remembered the pledge of allegiance and aimed to the left. Dolores pulled the trigger, then pulled it again. Geraldo screamed like a woman and Dolores kept pulling the trigger. Geraldo continued screaming until finally Dolores threw the gun down on the ground and plunked herself next to Geraldo in the dirt.

"What happened to the gun, Geraldo?" said Dolores.

Geraldo rolled his face out of the dirt, brushing twigs out of his hair and spitting out grains of dust.

"Goddamn it, Dolores, you could have killed me!"

"But the gun quit working, Geraldo. Why do you think it did that?" Dolores picked up the gun and began inspecting it as if she might know what to look for.

"Well now, goddamn it, Dolores, it probably jammed." Geraldo smoothed back his hair with both hands. "Where'd you get that thing, anyway?"

"At the Honest Deal Pawnshop in Bloomfield," said Dolores, rolling the gun from side to side in her hand.

Geraldo reached for the gun and looked at the price tag. "Well now, there ya go. A gun like that, a working gun, shoulda cost ya twice that. Pawnshops are like mechanics, honey. Women shouldn't deal with them unless they got a man standing there with 'em. You can't be too careful, Baby. Some people just ain't honest." With that, Geraldo put his arm around Dolores and the two of them drove home and lived happily ever after until the next time Geraldo staggered through the door with the smell of another woman's body trapped in his beard.

Dolores had pretty much given up on guns the night she sat at the El Nido Bar waiting for her husband to come through the door, so everyone figured that the gun-in-the-junkyard story would remain the benchmark for all succeeding disputes, unless, of course, Dolores actually ended up killing Geraldo at some future time.

As Salina and Yolanda were driving into the parking lot, Beany Moreno was walking toward the bar from her home across the El Nido Highway. She was not looking for customers this night; the season for deer hunters and fishermen was over and they had all returned to wherever they lived the rest of the year. Mainly she was bored and wanted to talk to someone besides her small daughter or aged parents. Beany was El Nido's only prostitute, but her devotion to her parents and daughter bartered acceptance from the town. Women looked the other way, purposely keeping themselves ignorant of Beany's source of extra income. Her work was seasonal, and she practiced a sort of shifting morality that did not allow her to step out to a car with the husband of someone she knew, making it easy for the women of El Nido to keep her as one of their own.

After Salina put her car into "park" and honked a hello, Beany waited for the women and all three entered the El Nido Bar laughing at Salina's joke about a man who finds a magic bottle with a genie inside who grants him one wish. The man wishes to be twice as smart as he already is, so the genie turns him into a woman.

The three women joined Della, Hortencia, and Dolores at the bar and they all gushed at what a coincidence it was to see each other since it was seldom that they were in the same place at the same time unless it was at church for a funeral. Dolores asked what the women had been laughing about as they entered the bar, so Salina told the joke again, and the women whooped and squealed until Lily teased that they would crack glassware if they kept it up.

After ordering a round for everyone, including Adolfo Flores and Hilario Armenta, who sat at the other end of the bar feeling invaded, Salina went to the jukebox and punched the numbers for Freddy Fender. "We're on our way to see him tonight," said Salina, smiling. All the women were impressed, and all except Della offered reasons why they hadn't bought tickets themselves.

"I forgot all about it," said Beany.

"I knew I would have to work," said Lily, setting up the drinks Salina ordered.

"I knew my husband wouldn't take me and he would be mad if I went without him," said Dolores.

"Who is Freddy Fender?" asked Hortencia. No one heard the old woman, so no one answered her and the women continued to swoon to the song on the jukebox.

Salina tried to pull Hilario and then Adolfo onto the tiny dance floor, but both men were unused to so many unescorted women in a bar and pleaded fatigue. She pirouetted away from the men and sang along with the song's refrain. *"Before the next teardrop falls . . ."*

"I luf dis es-song," said Yolanda.

"Do you think there are really any men who love their women like the words in the song?" asked Dolores, with a dreamy serenity in her voice.

"Oh, please," said Salina as she danced back to the bar to join the women, "they just say that stuff for the first five minutes so we'll stick around for a lifetime waiting to feel that good again."

"Geraldo used to be so romantic," said Dolores.

"Mi esposo también," offered Yolanda. "Pero, no más."

"I was happy when my husband stopped being romantic," said Hortencia with a shrug.

"Well," said Dolores, "maybe they'd appreciate us more if they knew the pain of having babies. Maybe then things would be different."

Beany said no, that wouldn't work. They would just whine louder and longer and the women would have to take care of them nonetheless. "You know what it's like when they have the flu or get a cut finger. No, I'll have the babies just so I don't have to listen to them complain," said Beany.

The women agreed, except Della, that yes, in the end it was easier to just have the babies themselves.

Salina raised her glass. "To having babies," said Salina, slopping warehouse-quality white wine onto the bar as she clinked the glasses of the women around her.

Adolfo and Hilario motioned for Lily and shoved the money for a six-pack across the bar and left. As the men closed the door behind them, the women laughed at their backs and chided them as cowards.

Outside, Bubbles De La Cruz struggled to slam the door to a '63 Ford Fairlane. He and Bloomfield Betty had stopped to buy a pint of Captain Morgan rum and their plans included nothing more than staying warm and sipping further into unconsciousness. They would find a place to drink their rum while telling each other stories of the past, and they would comfort each other with an outstretched hand or a hug that mingled their respective smells of alcohol and cigarettes, unwashed clothes, and barely washed flesh. Perhaps they would even make love, each pretending the act meant they had found a soul mate at last, and now that they'd found each other they would hold on and they'd make a life together, beginning in the morning.

But when morning came they would go back to being sad and confused friends, convinced that people like them don't have soul mates because God has forgotten them.

Before Bubbles could get the car door closed, Hilario and Adolfo passed by him and warned that there were only women in the bar, that the females were about to hold a witches' meeting where they would be burning dolls dressed as men and sacrificing male babies, and if he knew what was good for him he'd wait until Bloomfield to buy his bottle.

Bubbles studied the men through a blur, then narrowed his eyes as he pondered the odds of coming out alive. Putting his right index finger in the air as if delivering a proclamation, Bubbles concurred that, yes, women in numbers, particularly when concentrated in a small space, were a very frightening thing and only a stupid man would put himself in harm's way needlessly. It was on to Bloomfield for anesthesia.

Back inside the bar, Salina ordered another round and when everyone had a glass she lifted her drink and said, "Here's to birth control. If they'da had it when I was in high school, I'da had me a ball." The women clinked their glasses and Hortencia said, "From what I hear, you had a ball anyway. It was only by some miracle you didn't get pregnant." Salina scrunched her face at Hortencia but laughed right along with the rest of the women.

"Las babies are es-such a mee-ree-cals," Yolanda said softly.

"When I had my first child I really thought I was the first woman to do that," said Dolores. Oh yes, the women agreed, they felt quite the same way after having a baby.

"Actually, my first baby really *was* a miracle because they said she wasn't going to live. They said she had something wrong with her heart. So I prayed and prayed, y ¡mira!, my Sofía will graduate next June. I know that God cured her."

"Ah," belched Della, "the doctors just didn't know what they were saying. She probably wasn't sick at all to begin with."

"No, she was!" shrilled Dolores.

"Is OK," Hortencia patted Dolores's hand. "I believe in miracles. I have always believed that one happened to me once." All of the women, except Della, who rolled her eyes, encouraged Hortencia to tell about the miracle.

"When I was a little girl, about five years old, my father died," said Hortencia. She looked up to the ceiling as if the facts written in her memory would be printed there. "Yes, it was near that time that I found my mother sitting in front of the house crying. I thought she was crying because she had just lost my father, but, come to find out years later, that wasn't it at all. She was crying because there wasn't anything to eat in the house. I remember we'd had sweet corn and tortillas for breakfast that morning. What I did not know was my mother had fed me and my four brothers and sisters the last of the food without eating anything herself."

The women sat quietly listening to Hortencia's story, each of them recalling a time when there were only tortillas and a little of something else set on the table to eat.

"I guess she didn't know what to do," continued Hortencia, "so she called all of us together and said we should go for a walk. I think she was hoping there might be some asparagus still growing along the ditch bank, or at least some mint leaves for tea." Hortencia took a long breath. "I still like mint tea," said Hortencia, wetting her lips with the tip of her tongue.

"We took our walk and returned with some skinny asparagus shoots and some bug-eaten mint leaves, and left them on the kitchen table. My mother was so tired, she lay across the bed and fell asleep. Hours later, mis hermanos and me went in to wake her up, crying that we were hungry. She sat on the side of the bed and told us that we would have to fill our stomachs with tea that night. But we all began talking at once, all of us trying to tell her that there was plenty of food. She shook her head but allowed us to pull her to the kitchen anyway, where we told her to look inside the cold box. My brother, unable to wait for her to pull the handle, opened it for her and I watched as my mother's eyes grew to the size of plates. 'How could this be?' said my mother. There, inside the cold box, were two whole chickens, a pile of potatoes, a bundle of green beans wrapped in brown paper, and three quart-jars of milk. Under the table sat a sack of flour and a bucket of dried pinto beans." Hortencia stared at the top of the bar with tears clinging to her sparse gray lashes. "'It is all the food in the world,' my mother whispered."

All of the women sat very still for a moment or two. Then Della said, "It was just a neighbor, though, someone who knew your mother needed help."

Hortencia looked up at Della and opened her mouth to speak, but Beany did it for her. "That's kind of a miracle too, though, isn't it? I mean, that they knew she needed help. And then wanted no thanks."

"It could have been an angel that told the neighbor to go and put the food, and that would certainly qualify it as a miracle," said Lily.

"What exactly *are* the qualifications for a miracle?" said Salina.

"The Holy Father in Rome keeps a list of things that he says are miracles, and you can mail away for the list, and I know for a fact that having an angel tell you to go do something nice is a miracle," said Dolores.

All the women outvoted the shake of Della's head with their own testimonies to what qualified as a miracle and agreed that Hortencia's family had indeed experienced a supernatural event, teetering right there on the precipice of being an actual miracle.

Dolores said that now that she thought about it, she was sure she'd had a miracle too. "I'd forgotten all about this. That's funny," mused Dolores, "I told myself I'd never forget."

"Tell us, tell us," chimed the women.

"I was driving back from Gallup. I was so tired and yet I was too afraid to pull over. It was night, and you know how deserted it is along that road. I was afraid that if someone found me asleep in the car they might, you know, do God-knows-what and no one would have seen a thing. There's nothing out there, you know, nothing at all along that one stretch. So I kept driving. I didn't realize I'd fallen asleep at the wheel until I felt the hand." Dolores put her own hand down to a place just above her knee. "A strong hand had taken hold of my leg and shaken it so hard that I could still feel the hand on my thigh after I'd come awake and swerved

away from almost driving into a culvert." She shook her leg. "I felt
a hand," said Dolores with finality. "I can feel it now," and rubbed
the place on her leg where she said she felt the hand.

Della had been fishing in her empty glass for a piece of ice and
without looking up, said, "Sí, tonta, tú tienes una hand on your
leg. It is your own."

She popped the piece of ice into her mouth as if she had delivered the last word on the subject.

"Goddamn it, Della . . ." began Dolores.

"Escucha, you prob'ly just hit a bump and your leg hit the shifting stick. Or your purse fell against your leg. Who knows?" Little
bursts of water from the crunching ice flew from Della's mouth
and landed on the bar as she spoke.

"The car was an automatic," said Dolores through clenched
teeth. "And I know what I felt, Della Mondregal. I felt a hand shaking my leg just like I'm going to shake your face if you don't stop
talking all sour grapes." Della went back to digging in her glass for
ice cubes with a curve on her lips like that of a mother who'd just
listened to a fish story from a child.

"I've got one too," said Beany. "I mean, I think it's a miracle."

Just at that moment the door to the bar swiveled open and
brought with it a tiny woman wrapped in drab, ill-fitting clothing. Shivering and rubbing chapped hands together, Maggie Serna
smiled in the direction of the women without raising her eyes to
look at them.

"Buenas noches," said the woman, giving a nod of her head.
The women greeted her and wondered out loud what had brought
her to the El Nido Bar on such a cold night when they had never
seen her there before—even in good weather. Maggie looked every
day of her forty-two years. The only makeup she still owned was
tangled in broken shoestrings, used rubber bands, and clean but
crumpled tissue at the back of a crowded drawer in the bathroom.
She seldom looked up when she was noticed in town doing her
errands and seldom spoke more than a polite "buenos días" when
approached. But this night Maggie looked around the bar, and

seeing only women, delivered the only joke she'd made in three blue moons: "Oh sí, ya comprendo," she said, "the bodies of the men are piled in the back. Where are the shovels to bury them?" Maggie feigned a search of the corners of the bar with her eyes and pretended to look under a nearby table.

The women laughed and told her to sit down.

"No puedo, señoras, I must return to my children. I have come only to buy some sodas. I promised them sodas, then forgot them when I was in town. I haven't had peace since I showed up without them."

The women told her that they were discussing miracles and that Beany was just about to tell them about her own.

"Well, maybe I can stay for just one miracle," said Maggie, and she leaned against a stool near the door.

"I don't really know if it *was* a miracle," said Beany, suddenly shy, "but it kind of feels like one because my little girl is still alive."

The women leaned closer to Beany, encouraging her to go on.

"Well, it was so strange. You know how the television never works out here?" They all nodded and agreed that the reception was unpredictable at best. "This one day," continued Beany, "I had turned it on to see if I could get anything on the stupid thing. I was going to do my ironing. I was even willing to settle for the news, and wouldn't you know, that's what was on. There was this man showing this hemlock, no the Hemler, no—¿Cómo se llama? What is it where you save someone from choking to death by grabbing them around the middle from behind?"

"I know, I know!" called out Salina, bouncing on her barstool. But before she could say the words, Della answered, "The Heimlich maneuver." Salina glared at Della, but Della paid no attention, so Salina put her elbow back on the bar, resting her chin in her hand, and continued to listen to Beany's miracle.

"Yes, that's it," said Beany, "the himlack. So this man comes on and he showed how you grab a person, and if you do it just right, the thing that's choking them flies out of their mouth. He said you can tell if somebody is really choking because they can't make any sound. They can't cough, or wheeze, or nothing. He said if the person can make any kind of sound, they're probably going to be all right. I watched the man, and wouldn't you know, as soon as he finished showing the hemlock manure, the television went snowy again."

"Well," said Della, with a scowl, "there might be a miracle in there somewhere if you learned how to pronounce 'Heimlich.'"

The women looked daggers at Della while Beany went on with the story.

"No, no, that's not the end. Later that day I was still ironing and my little girl came saying she was hungry, so I gave her an orange. I had peeled it and pulled it into sections and she sat down at the table to eat it. I could see her from where I stood at the ironing board, but mostly I wasn't looking up, but just ironing away, thinking of nothing, you know how you do."

All the women nodded, affirming that they knew exactly the sorts of things women think of when they iron.

"Then it hit me," said Beany. "I didn't hear anything. I looked up and my little girl was sitting so still. I mean, I never realized before that day how much noise a person makes just by breathing, just by being alive. And when the noise is gone it's sooooooo silent."

The women bent even closer to Beany.

"I remember thinking as I walked to my daughter, 'Ay Dios, I hope this works. I hope that man knew what he was talking about.' Her mouth was open but nothing could come out. So I grabbed her from the chair and put my arms around her from behind."

"¿Dónde? Wher' deed ju put ju arams?" asked Yolanda.

"Right here," said Beany, and showed everyone where they should put their arms to save the life of a person who is choking.

"Then you pull back, kinda quick, kind of snapping the knot you've made with your hands right there in front, and that makes the extra air force out whatever got caught."

The women were in awe of Beany's expertise.

"The orange piece came flying out of my daughter's mouth. And she started crying because it scared her, and I started crying because I was so scared—and then relieved—and my mom came from the bedroom because of the noise, and she started crying because we were crying, but she didn't know why. And my father slipped out the back door when he heard all of us crying."

The women, including Della, threw their heads back laughing at the scene Beany painted in their minds.

"I don't know what I would have done if I hadn't seen that man on television, though," said Beany, shaking her head at the very thought. The women had their laugh, then stared at Beany and shook their heads with the same slow terror of being unprepared to save a child's life.

"Do you think it was a miracle?" asked Beany. "Would that be considered a miracle?"

"Well," huffed Hortencia, "it's every bit a miracle as finding food in the cold box."

"Yes, I think that's a miracle," said Dolores with her eyebrows knitted together.

"No doubt about it," confirmed Salina. "I mean, the television came on just long enough for you to see that man, and then it was gone."

"Oh, jes," said Yolanda. "Este es un mee-ree-cal."

Maggie, too, agreed by slowly, pensively nodding her head. Maggie believed that any situation in which a child is saved from harm is a miracle, and in some way involved the intervention of angels. She believed this because she was raising seven children and was resigned that she could not be everywhere at once, so she said her prayers every morning and gave most of the credit for her children's safety to God.

The women were nodding at each other and all speaking at once, and each of them was smiling at Beany or reaching out to touch her hand when Della screamed above the din, "But what does it mean! Does it mean God knew her little girl was going to choke? And if she was going to choke and he wanted Beany to save her, then why have her choke at all?"

For a moment no one had an answer and they hated Della for asking the question. "Pero es still un mee-ree-cal, ¿que no?" said

Yolanda. "Of course it is," and "Oh yes, I think so," and "A child was saved; that's all that matters," all the women chimed at once.

"My gosh, look at the time," said Salina. "We'll miss Freddy Fender."

"Don't go," pleaded Hortencia.

"Stay another five minutes," said Beany.

"I'll buy the next round," said Dolores.

"Oh, what the heck," said Salina, looking at Yolanda for approval. "We'll only miss the first band and we can see the Latin Express anytime down at the Four Queens." Lily got up from her stool behind the bar and began mixing fresh drinks.

"Well, I know I have to go," said Maggie, "before the kids start walking the three miles down here to get their own sodas."

The women told Maggie good-bye, then turned to each other asking who had the next miracle.

"Well," said Lily, "it didn't happen to me, but I read in the newspaper just the other day that a woman was trapped in her car for hours after it went off the highway. It happened somewhere back East. And it was real cold. And where her car went off the road was where no one would stop. And the road wasn't traveled much. And do you know what happened next?"

The women shook their heads, even Della, because of course they did not know what had happened next.

"A man ran out of gas right there where the woman's car had gone off the road. And when he got out of the car he could hear her moaning. And so he walked to where he heard the moaning and saved her life. And I think that was a miracle."

The women nodded all together again. "Oh yes, amazing," and "Isn't that something?" and "Gracias a Dios." The women were very impressed with this miracle even though it hadn't happened to anyone they knew.

"Well, the idiot had to run out of gas somewhere," said Della without looking up.

"Cabrona Della, do you have a stone in your chest instead of a heart?" said Dolores with her eyes narrowed.

"I just know that only men are stupid enough to run out of gas on a deserted road," Della shot back.

"What's that got to do with anything? And besides, it didn't have to be that deserted road, at that particular spot, now, did it?" said Salina as she put her hand on her hip.

"You just don't understand coincidence. None of you. These are coincidences that turn out doing something good for somebody. That's all." Della's jaw clamped down.

It was a good thing Della had known these women all her life or she might have been called some names she wouldn't be able to forgive. Each of them had something to say about Della's disbelief, and they all said it at once.

"What about the hand?" said Dolores.

"It didn't have to be that road," said Lily.

"We never knew who brought the food," said Hortencia.

"The TV only worked long enough . . ."

Della put up her hands to fend off the assaults, then screamed more loudly than all of the women, "What about when the miracle means you die!"

The women looked at Della as if she had suddenly begun to speak in tongues.

"Della," said Dolores with exasperation, "What the hell are you talking about?"

"I'm talking about what about when the woman in the car doesn't get saved because some fool runs out of gas, and she just dies. Isn't that a coincidence too that nothing happened to save her? It's simple. Sometimes you make it through something and sometimes you don't. Look at the stuff that people should have made it through and they didn't. Is that a reverse miracle? And what's so goddamned great about living anyway? You get told all this stuff about how wonderful the kingdom of God is, but nobody's in a hurry to get there, are they? If it's so goddamned wonderful, how come we all don't line up praying to die as soon as possible? If all that shit is true, we ought to feel sorry for people who live through accidents and be happy for those who don't!" Della slammed her fist on the bar.

No one said a word until Hortencia waved an arm and stirred her hand in the air and said, "Bueno, otros tragos para todos. I'm buying." Then everything was quiet again. Lily got up to get the drinks, but before she could scoop ice into the first glass, the phone rang. All the women jumped because the quiet had filled the room to overflowing.

Lily reached for the receiver and smiled at the women as she did. "This is one time I can tell whoever it is that her husband really isn't here." No one laughed.

"El Nido Bar," said Lily into the receiver. She listened for a moment. "Maggie?" Lily put her hand over the mouthpiece and turned to the women as she mouthed Maggie's name. "Wait, wait, slow down. Now what happened to Jesse?" The women at the bar raised their heads, all of them looking at Lily, trying to read her face. They all knew that Jesse was Maggie's youngest son, perhaps three years old now. Women in El Nido were raised to believe that all the children of their town belonged to everyone. It was common for women to wipe the noses of other women's children, scold them if the mother failed to notice some wrongdoing, or comfort them if they happened to be the one closest. Anything that had to do with the children of El Nido was the business of all. And now these women were watching Lily's face, holding their breath.

"You're kidding," said Lily into the phone.

"What?!" clamored the women. Lily put up her hand to keep them quiet. "Yes, yes, Beany's still here. Yes, I'll tell her. Yes, I'll tell them all. Yes, they're all still here. Yes, honey, now don't cry anymore."

The women were ready to jump over the bar. Lily gave them a smile to calm them and watched the breath they had been holding flow from their chests. "Yes," said Lily, "I know. I'll tell them right now."

Lily hung up the phone. "That was Maggie."

"Goddamn it, Lily, we know that. What *happened*?" Dolores wanted to hit her.

"Jesse. He was trying to swallow a piece of meat. They'd had dinner and Maggie hadn't cleared the food away yet. Jesse went back to the table when no one was looking and took a piece of meat. He was blue when Maggie found him. She did the Heimlich maneuver and it worked. She was crying because it scared her so badly and she was so happy it worked. She said if she hadn't forgotten the sodas, hadn't come in here tonight, hadn't waited to hear Beany's miracle, she would not have known how to do the Heimlich maneuver and save her son's life."

Beany made the sign of the cross as rivulets of black mascara ran down her cheeks. Salina and Yolanda hugged each other. All the women began hugging each other exclaiming, "¡Ay Dios Madre!" and "¡Gracias a Dios!" and "Can you believe it?"

Then the women looked at Della, her face buried in her hands, and Dolores put an arm around her heaving shoulders. Dolores held on to Della, offering a safe place for her to cry, while the other women reached out to pat a shoulder, stroke an arm, touch her hair, or smooth away a rumple in her clothing.

"Can we keep just this one miracle, Della? Just this one?" Dolores said gently into Della's hair.

With her hands still covering her face, Della nodded her head.

"Yes," she said through the lace of her fingers. "Oh, yes."

louds roiled and rumbled over Manzanares Mesa. Needle-thin lightning bolts lit up, shimmied a teaser dance, then disappeared behind veils of gloom. The gathering storm lent a gunmetal hue to the late September afternoon, with only gradual darkening of gray shades to portend the sun's slipping below the horizon.

The clouds turned the inside of the empty El Nido Bar into a cocoon—quiet, dark, solitary. Lily was content to listen to the silence, even prayerful the dark day might send customers past the bar and safely to their homes where they might sequester themselves against the coming storm. But she knew, too, that no matter the weather, there would always be people who needed a drink—and they wanted witnesses. They came to bars to become numb and invisible, yet wanted someone to notice. They came in good times or sad. They came because it was a place to go where they felt comfortable with their habits.

What Lily had not expected was that the next person through the door would be Jesus.

Carried by Napoleón Cabanero, Jesus wore velvet and a crown of thorns. Droplets of blood diluted with sweat spread across his brow, trickled down his cheeks, and stained the white shroud covering his chest. His eyes were turned upward, almost comically crossed, in an agonizing invocation to God the Father. Shafts of light beamed from a shiny cross held within a purple valentine-shaped heart. There was a portrait lamp clipped to the frame of the picture and an electrical cord snaked along behind Napoleón as he entered the bar.

Lily said nothing as Napoleón straddled a bar stool. He ordered a Schlitz and a shot of Wild Turkey, and held on to Jesus with one enormous arm. Lily gave him the order without delay or conversation and began washing the clean glasses of customers who hadn't been there yet. She pretended that at some time or another all patrons of the El Nido Bar sat with a picture of their favored deity resting on a knee. Napoleón was not the sort of man you asked questions. He was huge, well over six feet tall, and built like a well-conditioned wrestler. Lily had heard he was impervious to pain and psychic when it came to dodging blows. In spite of the sweet appearance of his smooth, cherublike complexion, he was a brooding drunk, too intelligent for the poverty and ignorance he'd been born into, and the frustration had given his mind a turn.

Napoleón pushed a quarter of his change back toward Lily and said, "Un pobre no más."

It was the song most played on the decrepit jukebox. A beautiful song about a poor man who meets a pretty woman and they fall in love. Caring nothing for the things he cannot give her, the woman wishes only to hold the man close to her. The literal translation of the refrain was that he is "a poor man no more" because of this woman's love. It didn't occur to Lily to tell Napoleón to get off his bar stool and go play the song himself, and it wasn't fear that kept her from telling him so. He looked incapable. As if the huge man had done battle, and now, wounded and troubled, sat in a safe spot to catch his breath and ponder his next move.

Lily took the quarter and walked noiselessly to the jukebox. After punching in the numbers, she avoided going back behind the bar. She silently rearranged chairs, picking them up instead of dragging them, and setting them down within an inch from where they had been. Napoleón paid no attention; he paid no attention when the whine of El Nido's only fire engine turned into the dirt parking lot and ruined the song's refrain.

Napoleón and Jesus had neglected to fully close the door, and now Lily walked out of it as if the destination of the fire truck were the most important thing she needed to know at that moment. As Lily walked out, Beany Moreno was turning into the doorway and the two women collided, almost bouncing off each other, then both instinctively grabbing onto each other for support. Because Lily was almost eight inches taller, Beany got a faceful of Lily's chest, while Lily breathed in a mouthful of moussed hair. They were still laughing and begging pardon when the fire truck came to a stop on the road leading behind the bar.

"Gotta match?" grinned Beany. She took hold of Lily's hand as if they were two little girls running after the ice cream wagon and said, "Let's go see."

Lily allowed herself to be led around the corner of the building, where the two women were immediately transfixed by the sight of a dilapidated two-room house overwhelmed by flames. The volunteer firemen pulled hoses and shouted orders at each other, but their mission was not to save the house. It was too late for that. The fire had turned the building into a gyrating mirage as it gulped the disappearing outline of four walls. The only thing the men could do now was wet down anything close enough to catch fire.

"Helluva fire for roasting chile," said Beany, laughing, but Lily barely caught the words before she turned away and walked back inside the bar.

Napoleón continued to hug Jesus to his chest and drained the last of the Schlitz while the scratched record on the jukebox hic-cupped the word "pobre."

"It's . . . it's your house, Napoleón," said Lily gently. Napoleón stared into the mirror bolted to the wall behind bottles of liquor. There seemed to be no air in his lungs when he answered, "Yo sé, mujer. I know."

He stepped off the barstool, pulling himself up to his full height, and walked past Lily as if she weren't standing there, and stepped out the door. Lily followed behind him, watching from

a safe distance as he buckled Jesus into the passenger seat of the
'72 Chevy Nova. He settled himself behind the steering wheel
and drove away without looking back. The electrical cord hung
outside the passenger door, the metal prongs igniting sparks as
he turned onto the pavement.

Beany watched him drive away too. Shaking her head and
smiling grimly, she said, "That man has always been loco-motion.
Hey, you got any Marlboros in the machine?"

It was a fair question. Vendors didn't like coming to the El
Nido Bar, and when they did, it was usually on a Monday morning, early, prearranged with the owners. The reputation of the
place unnerved them, and even the locals were hard-pressed to
predict when it might erupt into a re-creation of Sam Peckinpah's
The Wild Bunch with Spanish subtitles. The vendors had heard
tales of shootings and stabbings and knew that police never drove
Highway 46 east to El Nido unless there was blood involved. There
was no rush to the crime scene before evidence was destroyed
because someone would still be there, ready to provide details of
the assault and directions to the perpetrator's house.

In reality, the El Nido Bar had outlived a reputation garnered
at the turn of the twentieth century when the territory was lawless.
The reputation was brought to a crescendo in the 1950s while the
Navajo Dam was under construction. The project hired a few locals
to do the lowest-paid chores, but mainly shipped in its own crew.
This made the people of El Nido feel cheated out of badly needed
work. Worse, the crew was mostly Anglo. The job site was an edgy
atmosphere as it was, but then the Anglos expected to drink and
play pool alongside men whose jobs they had taken. It was a brawl
waiting for the starter gun to go off. And it went off every Friday and
Saturday night for six years while the dam was being built.

Once the dam was completed and the Anglos left, assaults took
back their rightful place between friends or neighbors, sometimes
among family. The reasons were as old as humankind itself: the
attention of a woman, a bad debt, a long-standing feud over water

or land boundaries, putting another man's machismo into question, somebody's brother having beaten somebody else's cousin three months earlier—all were recognized as valid provocation. Simply add alcohol and stir until bruised. When it was all over, everybody was sorry. Or they weren't sorry one bit and when next the two scufflers stood in the same bar, the same rooster routine played out again.

Although the dam had been finished for more than twenty years, it remained a bad idea for an Anglo man who wasn't a local to be in the bar on a Friday night, downright stupid if he played pool, starkly suicidal if he won the game.

Beany checked the cigarette machine and settled for Winstons. Lily asked her what she was drinking and she answered that a Pepsi with a glass of ice would do just fine.

It was watching the ravenous flames devour a bereft building as if it were nothing more than a spare morsel, or maybe it was watching the mighty Napoleón caressing Jesus, his eyes destitute and houseless, that sent shudders of loneliness through Lily's body. Whatever the cause, Lily welcomed Beany's chatter about the price of stamps going up again, and that her little girl was learning to talk. Lily listened with half attention as she cleared away the mortal evidence of Jesus's visit, then realized that Beany was asking her a question.

"I said, 'just moved here,' right?" Then, without waiting for an answer, and her head tilted to one side, Beany added, "Why here?"

"Long story," answered Lily with a smile, and didn't offer to go on. Beany accepted the finality of the words with a nod of her head. A moment passed between the women, and it was during that moment that Lily decided she liked Beany.

"When we were watching the fire, you said something about roasting chile. What did you mean?" asked Lily.

"It's the only way," piped Beany. "Used to be that all the women roasted chile outside over an open fire. Now many have taken to doing it in the bottom of the oven." Beany shook her head as if the practice was a travesty. "Doesn't taste the same."

Lily watched Beany tear the filter off a Winston and light the jagged end.

"More work, though," said Beany, blowing out the match with blue smoke. "And you could burn out the temperature element in the oven," said Beany with authority.

The women talked more about roasting chile and how it was best to peel off the seared outside skin as soon as the pod cooled down. Some women freeze the chile with the skin still on and that just meant they'd have to deal with it later, Beany said.

"Tell you what. Come the fall, y si Dios quiere, we're both still alive, I'll show you how to roast chile the right way."

"See dose carry?" said Lily.

Beany threw back her head, showing black molars as she laughed. "If God wants it so," explained Beany, and she taught Lily, syllable by syllable, how to say the expression.

"Gotta run, Angla. I have people to feed . . . laundry to do . . . where's my lighter . . ."

⸺ ◆ ⸺

I f there was a kinder, more feminine rendition of Beany's name, Lily never knew it. Everyone just called her Beany. When first meeting her, people often thought that Beany was short for something else like Benita or Bernadette. But among Beany's twelve brothers and sisters there was already a Benita and a Bernadette; everyone called them Benny and Bernie.

None of the Morenos might have been mistaken for attractive, even when viewed through a kind eye. They all had forgettable faces like those in a crowd scene on a picture postcard. Beany had not escaped the Moreno sludge-colored hair or sallow complexion. Behind plastic tortoiseshell glasses she wore "Lightning Blue" eye shadow on transparent eyelids supporting sporadic lashes painted with "Midnight Black" mascara. On thin lips eternally poised at the edge of laughter, Beany penciled fuchsia lip liner, then colored inside the lines with magenta lip rouge.

It was a hideous combination, an intolerable look on anyone other than Beany and women like her. On Beany it was the look of comfort—one of those women who wear dangly earrings with high hair and clothes too tight who are always taking care of someone else. One of those women who will cry with you when you tell them stories of your childhood, then laugh without derision when you confide silly mistakes and faulty decisions.

Life was funny to Beany, even ridiculous. She laughed at it instead of blaming it. Without having read a book since high school, or ever having left El Nido in thirty-two years, Beany often threw her head back in raucous laughter and challenged those around her that they had not been paying attention. Hadn't they learned that life is a comedy and we all take turns being the punch line? Envy no one, said Beany. Everyone pays. Everyone gets a turn at the good; no one escapes the bad.

It did not sound jaded coming out of Beany's mouth; it was more like a philosophy for acceptance and a formula for sustaining sanity.

She laughed in the face of anyone who tried to cheat her. "Why you want to make yourself look stupid?"—which, of course, took the cheater off guard. "Oh sí, yo comprendo. You think I am the one who is stupid. See how stupid you are."

Beany laughed at her own foibles with ease. If she dropped the ember from a cigarette onto a shirt, she shrugged it off with a sigh as she stared at the burn hole and gave her head a slow shake. "This shirt don't look good on me no more." Back rocked Beany's head with mouth spread wide and a laugh that filled up the room.

She had tried night classes at the community college in Farmington, a seventy-mile round-trip on Monday and Wednesday evenings. She was doing well in the secretarial courses until the transmission in her '63 Pontiac started slipping, so driving along

the shoulder in second gear into Farmington took three times as
long, and, according to Sheriff Max, that was completely against the
law. The painted line delineating the shoulder from the highway
was not available as an extra lane, even in times of transmission
trouble, explained Sheriff Max. It was just a matter of time before
some drunk or truck driver would come up on her flank as she
whined along at twenty-eight miles an hour and pull an unintended
pit maneuver, said Max. Of course, he then had to explain what a
pit maneuver was.

"Por último, Señora," said Max, "Manejar tan despacio es muy
peligroso. I do not want to be the one called to the scene."

Beany quit the classes and got a job at Farmer's Market in
Bloomfield. She traded several goats to Beto Archuleta in a bargain to have him fix the transmission. After the transmission was
rebuilt, the clutch flapped helplessly against the floorboard, leaving Beany beside the road with only fifteen minutes to make it to
work. Beto said he would fix the clutch if he could have the fenders off the rusting 1946 Chevy pickup belonging to Beany's father.
After the clutch's tension was restored and once again able to help
the gears move through their pattern, the alternator sucked the
battery dry and then there were two things to replace.

Although the manager of Farmer's Market had no qualms about
Beany's work and said he was sorry to let her go, he explained that
he needed reliable people with cars that ran more than one day
in row.

⸺•⸺

F or the rest of September and into October, Beany came into
the bar occasionally to buy cigarettes, sip on a soda, and
exchange forgettable gossip. It never occurred to Lily to ask what
Beany did for a living; she assumed she was married because she
talked about her daughter and a man named Alfredo who had
beautiful green eyes and bought her nice things. If she came into

the bar at night, she simply sailed through with a wave, and the next time Lily looked around, she'd be gone. Beany's visits began to change as autumn moved deeper into winter.

Late October and all of November is a time of prosperity for El Nido. Fishermen pour in from every corner of New Mexico for the salmon run at Navajo Dam and spend lots of money on groceries, fishing gear, gasoline, microwave burritos, and of course, beer. They leave their wives and children at home and pull their limit out of the San Juan while drinking beer with buddies away from the chastising eyes of family. After the salmon run come the deer hunters. The activities remain the same.

The locals were tolerant of the invaders as long as they didn't try to make the El Nido Bar their own—or win at pool. Confrontations were uncommon during the hunting season, usually never progressing past what Lily called the rooster stage—two men standing with their chests puffed out and bobbing their heads at each other in an invitation to strike. Most of the time a simple "You guys knock it off; this is a nice place" provoked enough laughter that the situation defused itself.

During this time Lily began to see Beany in the bar more often. She strolled in wearing her size three Wranglers and extra eye shadow, waving at Lily over the heads of men talking about rifles and the one that got away. Before anyone noticed the sleight of hand, Beany had joined a cluster of hunters crowded around the bar. It was inevitable that one of them offered his seat and bought her a drink. Whatever the man was drinking was Beany's favorite. She laughed at every joke, no matter how trivial, and agreed with every opinion no matter how slanted. After a while, the man and Beany were no longer sitting at the bar, and his buddies were snickering as the two slipped out the heavy wood door.

Sometimes the man came back in looking angry and telling his buddies it was time to go. If the man was alone, he might not come back in at all. Sometimes Beany came back in alone and headed straight for the bathroom. Sometimes the man and Beany came back in together, holding each other around the waist, looking somewhat disheveled and laughing like old friends.

When the hunting season was over and before the winter holidays began, the bar settled back into a slow shuffle of regular customers, and again Beany began to visit Lily in the empty afternoons.

During one of their sessions of idle conversation, Beany stubbed out a Camel cigarette and said, "It's not like I'm a real prostituta, Angla. I just ask 'em for what they can afford—kinda like donations. And all according to what they want."

Then Beany had thrown her head back in bawdy laughter and said, "There are certain things no man should get for free, ¿verdad, angla?" The laughter gamboled against the adobe walls of the cantina, then seeped in and stayed there. With no words to offer, Lily gave a half smile and pretended to check the amount of liquor left in a vodka bottle.

Beany tore the filter off another Camel and grew quiet. "But sometimes the men get angry. I don't understand." The confusion behind her eyes and the slow shake of her head made her statement believable.

"Why don't you just tell them from the jump it's gonna cost 'em?" said Lily.

Beany opened her mouth and inserted a pinky finger in search of a stray piece of tobacco. Finding it, she flicked the bitter flake into the abyss of the bar's cracked linoleum floor.

"I'm not so pretty, this I know. And not so young," said Beany, looking into the mirror behind the bar. "It's better if I get 'em worked up to where, you know . . . to where they don't want to stop before I ask 'em. ¿Comprendes?"

"Sí amiga, yo comprendo," said Lily, using some of the Spanish she'd been learning. Then both women fell silent until Beany picked up her cigarettes and told Lily she'd see her again soon.

The following year it seemed as if summer had saved its most scorching days for September, the Navajo medicine men predicting warm days well into October. An Indian summer is always welcome in northwest New Mexico; it means bumper crops from gardens and an extra cutting of hay. It means flamingo sunsets swirling over lavender mesas at twilight until all the colors mix themselves up and fall into the indigo of night. For Lily, it meant it was time to learn how to roast chile outside over an open fire. Beany had not forgotten her promise.

The women dug a small pit in front of Lily's rented trailer and placed stones in a circle around it. Wood was crowded into the pit and Beany propped a wire rack across the stones.

It was the first time Lily had detailed her journey to El Nido to anyone she'd met since arriving, explaining that she had come to be where she was in very much the same way she'd come to be just about everywhere else she'd ever been—there seemed to be no place else to go at the time. Lily left Ventura, California, because a friend she'd known from childhood told her to come to Albuquerque. Before that, she had left Los Angeles to get away from people who talked to themselves in the streets; men who claimed they were photographers, actors, and writers but lived in studio apartments with sparse furnishings; and because of an unexplainable feeling that whatever she was looking for wouldn't be found there. Before that, she had left her husband in Seattle because she was afraid she'd kill him if he opened his mouth one more time to tell her a lie. Before that, she had left Fresno when she was seventeen years old because her second stepfather couldn't seem to stop telling her she wasn't wanted in his home and her mother never contradicted him.

The friend was right about Albuquerque. She liked it until the friend stole a necklace and denied it and had Lily apologizing for accusing her. Then Lily walked in on the friend having sex with the same man Lily had been having sex with and realized that California didn't have a monopoly on people trying to figure out who they were. Lily didn't much care about the boyfriend; it was the way the two of them snickered at her shock and asked if she wanted to join them. She found that she could no longer look at the friend's face without wanting to dig fingernails into it, so she packed her car and headed north. Although too small for her to wear, folded within one of Lily's suitcases was the friend's favorite blouse.

Lily headed north and then turned east onto the last highway before the Colorado border. She drove until she saw a FOR RENT sign and a HELP WANTED sign, both within the same mile.

The first day Lily unloaded her suitcases into her one-person mobile home she drove to Jack Lobato's Grocery and bought a couple of beers and a pack of cigarettes. She sat outside with a beer, watching the buildup to a magnificent sunset while she cried and talked to herself and cut the friend's blouse into pieces small enough to use as confetti.

Beany nodded with compassion and offered a sincere "¡Qué lástima!" at each of Lily's moves.

As the women sat before the fire, tears were replaced with elaborate plans for revenge against those who had caused the most pain and it wasn't long before the quiet of the land quivered with the sound of women's laughter.

"I'll help you, Angla. We'll invite all the people who have hurt our feelings to a party and then we'll blow up the building. After all, these are people who will always hurt people's feelings, ¿que no? The world is better off without them."

"Beany, I don't know spit from shoe polish about explosives. We'd probably blow ourselves up first."

Beany thought this very funny, and with a screeching peal of laughter, agreed that maybe they should think of something else.

The women turned their attention back to the chile. Beany tore the filter off a Virginia Slim and offered the pack to Lily, who held up a hand and fished one of her own cigarettes out of a near-empty pack.

"This has not always been a place of laughter, Angla," said Beany. "Do you know the story of your little mesita?"

Lily admitted that she didn't, and encouraged Beany to go on.

"A small band of Hopi camped here one night. They were traveling back to their home after fishing in the San Juan, not far from here. Some Anglo soldiers found them in the night and slaughtered them, down to the last child." Beany rocked back on her hunches and lifted her chin into the air. "In September the winds cry like women."

Beany and Lily sat quietly for many minutes listening to the wind, but heard only the sound of blistering chile spitting seeds into the fire.

Beany told Lily about the married man, Alfredo, who was the father of her little girl. She confided her situation as if it was secret, so Lily treated it that way. It was months before Lily realized that she was the only one keeping the secret and that everyone else already knew, including Alfredo's wife.

Every Sunday the man told his wife a lie and came to visit, bringing money and love. He gave his daughter tiny silver bracelets and miniature turquoise earrings made by a genuine Navajo craftsman. Beany said the child raised and lowered her arm for minutes on end just to watch the bracelets slide along "her sweet brown skin." From the moment her father had first seen her, he had called her "La Preciosa," and he brought her the first pair of earrings and her first tiny bracelet when she was just a week old, Beany said.

The women settled into comfortable quiet for a few minutes until Beany popped up from her place at the fire and said, "Gotta run, amiga. I have to make dinner for my family, and the ironing is piled to the ceiling." She gathered half the roasted chile and quickly folded a blanket while mindlessly muttering a list of chores she needed to accomplish.

"My mom has her doctor's appointment tomorrow. Ay, Dios, and you know how it is. If you're going into Farmington for one thing you may as well get twenty things done, ¿que no? The groceries, el banco, take my mom to visit her sister—for two minutes, anyway. They are both so old you never know when it will be the last time they see each other. Fill the car with gas on the way home . . ."

Lily nodded that indeed the round-trip into Farmington meant an entire day of grocery shopping, appointments, and errands.

"I need to write my list . . . give the baby her bath. . . . I wonder if my brother could sit with my dad. Since the stroke it's hard to get him in and out of the car. . . . Where did I leave my lighter . . ."

Slamming the car door and waving an arm out the window, Beany drove away from the rented mobile home, calling to Lily, "Adiós, mi amiga. Hasta luego."

Lily waved at the dust flying behind Beany's 1968 Ford Galaxy, the back bumper tied to the car's frame with a strip of bailing wire, the sun glinting off the dented right rear door panel, and a muffler loud enough to warrant a ticket.

The hunting season came and went yet another time and again Beany came to the bar on the slow afternoons to smoke cigarettes, sip her soda, and laugh with Lily about the latest shenanigans of El Nido's young men and people of all ages who never seemed to learn better.

"¿Conoces a Dolores Álvarez? The one married to Geraldo Álvarez? He works at Montalvo's junkyard stripping parts from all the wrecked cars up there," said Beany.

Lily thought until she conjured a face to match the name.

"She has kind of bushy hair, right?"

"That's the one," said Beany. "Well, she went looking for Geraldo the other day with a gun and had it in her mind to kill him."

"My God, why?"

"She found a lipstick in the car and figured Geraldo was getting some on the side. Since she didn't know who the other woman was so she could her beat her up, she decided to kill Geraldo."

"So what happened?"

"Montalvo said she killed mostly distributor caps, a couple window shields, a side mirror, and missed Geraldo altogether before she ran out of bullets."

Lily pondered the very idea of someone pulling a gun on another someone and shooting real bullets, then said, "Well, I guess that's another divorce statistic."

"Oh no, mija, they are in love again this very day."

"Wha . . . ?" and both women began to laugh from the bottoms of their bellies.

Beany smoked another cigarette, then said it was time to go. "The baby will be awake from her nap. Tortillas to make . . ." And Beany continued naming off another list of her daily chores.

Lily stopped her before she got to the door. "I'm not going to work here anymore," said Lily.

"I know," smiled Beany. "You are going to marry Agustín Jácquez and live happily ever after."

"Do you really believe that can happen, living happily ever after?"

"Yes," said Beany, "I believe it happens. And I believe it should happen to you."

The two women smiled and Lily watched Beany move toward the door.

"But you'll come to see me at the house. I won't be at the bar anymore, so you'll stop by the house, won't you? We're going to roast chile together every year until we're very old, ¿que no?"

"Si, amiga," Beany assured, "we will see each other."

When spring came, Lily saw the man and Beany and La Preciosa walking along the ditch bank picking asparagus. In spite of the outdoor excursions, the child was dressed as she always was to receive her father on Sundays. A brightly colored frock, often velvet, ended just below her chubby thighs, and patent-leather shoes with lacy socks matching the dress made the child look like an ad for a children's store. The delicate silver and turquoise bracelets slid between her wrist and forearm as she bent to pick an asparagus shoot, then raised it to show her father.

Summer sneaked up on spring and Lily stopped working at the bar. She spent her days tending a vegetable garden, preoccupied with touching the places on her stomach where the child growing inside her tested the limits of its domain. The colors of the sunsets are different in summer: more orange than yellow, the mesas more purple than lavender. But when the colors of fall returned, so did Beany, and again the women sat in front of a fire sharing small secrets and watching green chile pods puff up. Beside Lily lay a rectangular laundry basket lined with a blanket and stuffed with a bed pillow. On top of the pillow Lily's son lay mesmerized by the hues of autumn and the sound of clement wind.

Beany pronounced the child perfect in every way and warned Lily not to listen to the experts too much. She said the child would be hungry for solid food before the suggested time and smiles were really smiles and not trapped gas. Later, Beany drove away waving a thin arm and laughing. She waved her arm out the window of her '64 Buick the whole way up the dirt road until she reached the highway and turned east.

⸻

It was Beany's sister Benita who came to the door on a frozen day in November. "Beany's dead," she said matter-of-factly, while still standing on the steps in the cold. A yelp escaped from Lily's throat and Benita said it again. Lily reached out for Benita and led her through the door and into the kitchen.

"How?" whispered Lily, "Tell me how."

"They killed her," said Benita.

"*Who* killed her?"

"They. Someone. They beat her. On the bluffs. Farmington."

Lily stared at Benita and Benita stared back, and then the two women embraced and patted each other's backs until Benita pulled away and brought out a wad of shredded tissue.

"She liked you," said Benita. "I thought you'd want to know before . . . you know, before the news . . . the radio."

"Yes," said Lily. "Yes, thank you."

Sitting down at the kitchen table and accepting the cup of coffee from Lily's hand, Benita said, "It was cold that night, you know." Lily didn't know which night Benita meant but she nodded her head anyway.

"They could have at least covered her up," said Benita.

Lily thought of Beany sitting out in front of the chile fire wearing a man's woolen shirt. Tiny as she was, she remembered, Beany chilled easily.

"Beany wouldn't have liked those people, those policemen finding her like that. Her breasts, you know . . . she always said they were too small. She was shy about that . . . did you know?"

Lily shook her head. "No, I didn't know that."

"They could have at least covered her up," said Benita. "No matter what, they shouldn't have left her like that. No matter . . . who she was. No matter . . ."

Benita left without telling Lily what she herself did not yet know, that Beany's body had lain out on the bluffs for three of the coldest days in November, that her forehead was crushed and her jaws smashed into viscous puddles, her mouth shaped like the gaping smile of a skeleton.

Eventually a man was arrested and the broken butt of a hunting rifle, thought to be the murder weapon, was taken into evidence. The man testified for himself at the trial. He hadn't realized what kind of woman she was. A money-grubbing woman. She fooled him. She laughed at him when he refused to pay. He lost his temper. He didn't know what happened to his mind. He had been drinking.

The man's wife brought their children and they all sat behind him every day of the trial, weeping. The man's attorney pleaded that there was a family at stake, small children to support. Beany's murder was an unfortunate blunder, something that happened while under the influence of strong drink, said the attorney. His client wasn't a danger to society. The man had responsibilities, entreated the attorney, and his family relied on him. It would be impossible for them to survive without him.

The court assessed Beany's life to be worth eighteen months in Santa Fe State Prison and told the man to do his time, then sin no more.

Beany's married man went to the Moreno house and took away La Preciosa, telling Beany's family he would give the child a good home. Six months later he brought her back, telling them he was afraid there would be nothing left of her if she stayed in his house. They were accidents, such terribly sad accidents, said the man. His son had accidentally shot out one of her eyes with a BB gun. His inattentive wife had allowed the child's arm to get caught in a dough-rolling machine. The doctors amputated it above the elbow. Now there was nowhere for the little silver bracelets to slide up and down, sobbed La Preciosa's father.

La Preciosa was left with two old people unable to care for themselves, much less a disabled child, so La Preciosa was passed from house to house among Beany's sisters. They loved her in the way that relatives feel obligated to love kindred blood, but burdened with their own broods and living day-to-day on the low pay of unskilled labor, all of them marked time until La Preciosa could be passed on to another home. In this way the years were used up until the girl turned eighteen and no one had to be responsible for the burden that Beany had left behind.

The house where Beany's parents lived fell into squalor as their children continually fussed over whose turn it was to care for the old people. The children felt that the old people needed help only every other day and they were so busy with their own lives that they agreed that a few things would simply have to go by the wayside. Weeds grew to the rim of windows. Crumbs and spills and the dirt from daily life turned to filth in the corners of floors, the tops of counters, and the inside of drawers. Food in the refrigerator sometimes dripped, then dried, then clung to the racks. The old people avoided bathing and changing clothes, especially in winter when they were afraid to catch a chill. Because of their incontinence they sometimes slept on soiled sheets, simply laying towels over damp spots until one of their children came to do laundry.

T he following autumn Lily's husband walked into their kitchen to find her roasting chile in the bottom of the oven.

"Why aren't you doing it outside?" he asked. "You always say it tastes better roasted outside."

"Not today," said Lily. "The wind sounds lonely today."

"It's the women in the wind," said Lily's husband nonchalantly. "Sometimes the wind sounds like women crying, doesn't it? It's a funny thing," he said, looking out the window.

The Legend of Booger Red

A t the turn of the twentieth century, New Mexico was not a state, and the hamlet of El Nido was not on the map of the New Mexico Territory. The people of El Nido liked it that way. They had no need for recognition, no desire to be found, and few aspirations beyond avoiding loss whenever possible.

Besides the Hopi Indians, who lived east of El Nido in what was later named the Carson Forest, and the Navajo, who lived anywhere they wanted until the United States corralled them onto a reservation straddling both sides of the Arizona–New Mexico border, El Nido residents had few neighbors. Most settlers of El Nido had sailed to the Americas from Spain or the Basque country, then followed the trail north from New Spain, later known as Mexico, toward the rumored cities of gold. Finding that the mirage was actually the glitter of bright sunlight off crystallized, grainy sandstone, they settled for drinking water and enough game to keep from starving. They stayed to raise sheep, some to farm the fertile land along the San Juan River, some to set up trade lines. Mostly they stayed because there was no way back, and at some point, the other riches New Mexico had to offer—mesas that turn the color of lavender at sunset, snow the color of blue diamonds when the moon shines full, all the stars in the universe concentrated into one patch of sky—all became important.

Along with the settlers were cowboys who wandered the country thinking they were looking for a home, bandits who wandered the country knowing they didn't want a home, and renegade Indians who wanted their home back. There was Mangas Coloradas, Red Sleeves, an Apache famous for always wearing a red shirt when he went out killing white people. There was Jimmy Two-Guns, named for obvious reasons, who was never outdrawn in more than thirty gunfights, but was beaten to death in his sleep by a woman he didn't love anymore.

Booger Red chose the western territories because the isolated towns and small cattle ranches were easy pickings for a man who made his living as a thief.

The people of El Nido had heard of Booger Red, but the first time anyone actually saw him was in the spring of 1910 when he fell off his horse in front of the Sandoval farm, suffering delirium caused by a gunshot wound to his back while riding away from an irate Colorado farmer who'd caught him in the act of stealing cattle. It was Prudencio Sandoval and his daughter Magdalena who found him and dragged him into the extra bedroom because it was kind of a law back then that if anyone fell off his horse in front of your house, you had to take care of him.

The Sandovals had the luxury of an extra bedroom because Magdalena was the youngest of nine children and the only one left at home. It was likely that she would remain at home for the rest of her life because the scarlet fever epidemic of 1892 had destroyed both her eardrums and she was deaf as a stone. She was too young at the time to have learned to talk much, so she was mute as well, except in times of rage or sorrow, and even then the sounds were more those of an animal. It was the same epidemic that killed four of Señora Madrid's children in one night, leaving alive only her baby Hortencia. The early morning hours ticking off the lives of her children left Señora Madrid with a permanent body tremor for the rest of her life. But that's another story.

After dragging Red into the extra room, the Sandovals sent for la Bruja Esmeralda, who arrived some hours later with her strongest potions and salves for which only she knew the recipes.

Several days later La Bruja left the Sandoval house knowing everything there was to know about the red-headed stranger recovering in the care of Magdalena.

He is the son of a San Patricio, announced La Bruja to the crowd that had followed her out of the church after Wednesday night Mass. There had seldom been so many souls at the midweek Mass as the night the rumor flew through town that La Bruja would be coming straight from the Sandoval house to the church. Now, after La Bruja said her prayers and began her exit, the crowd followed her outside like chicks after a hen.

La Bruja informed them that a hero's grandson—the grandson of a San Patricio—lay critically wounded at the Sandoval home and that they all must include him in their prayers. The crowd took a breath as they lowered their eyes and paid silent, collective homage to the legend of the San Patricios, Irishmen who had stood side by side with Spanish soldiers in the war against Los Estados Unidos over the very ground where they now stood.

La Bruja reminded them of a history they already knew. These Irish had come to the United States looking for work and an escape from starvation. Instead, they were turned away when looking for a job. They garnered no approval by joining the army and promising to put their lives on the line for God and country. Relegated to being slop handlers and used as pawns for the most dangerous strategies, they abandoned the U.S. army for the Mexican army, where they were welcomed and assimilated into Hispanic culture. After the war, which ended in defeat in 1848, the San Patricios retreated south, along with the rest of New Spain's army, and settled into a life of speaking Spanish and enjoying the respect of their countrymen. A celebration of recognition was created in their honor, and to this day the San Patricios are still celebrated in Mexico every year.

Let us all pray, said El Nido's residing witch.

In reality, Rufus Helmahn "Red" Mullerliele was a cattle-rustling thief who'd left behind the miserably cold winters of Minnesota, and his red hair was rooted in German stock rather than the Celtic genes of old Ireland. Back at the Sandoval place, when Red came out of his gunshot delirium, the first thing he saw was the smooth brown skin of Magdalena, her gray eyes set with concern. And the first thing Red did after seeing Magdalena was pull his gun on her and hold her captive while he sent her father for the priest. Red meant to marry Magda right there and then. He was fairly certain he'd died and God had misplaced his sin sheet, so, before his creator realized the mistake, Red meant to have his share of heaven with the angel Magdalena.

Magda was not the sort of woman to acquiesce simply out of fear. On this day, however, she allowed the big bad outlaw to think he was in charge. In actuality, Magda had decided Red's future long before he ever woke up, and the fact that Red held a gun on her to give her what she already wanted was the set of circumstances Magdalena had decided since dragging the ugly red-haired man through the door of her home. Although Magda had little experience with men her own age, she had already learned from living with her father and brothers that there is no end to the mileage a woman can get out of something she allows a man to think is his own idea.

Of course, evening Mass was over, the congregation had dispersed, and the priest had already gone to bed, so Magda's father returned to his house hoping the San Patricio's grandson would not shoot him for coming back empty-handed. Magda assured her father that the man had returned to his sleep and that all was well with the wedding taking place tomorrow.

And so it came true that the couple were married by the priest as Red lay fevered. Delirious or not at the ceremony, Red never regretted his commitment to the beautiful Magdalena. He didn't seem to mind that Magda was deaf and mostly mute. In fact, he thought she was just about perfect. Her blue-black hair was braided like silk rope, tied at the end with purple cloth where it fell against her knees, and watching her from behind as the braid bounced off each full hip as she walked prodded Red to whisper to himself that watching Magda was like getting drunk without the hangover.

As soon as Red was up and able to ride, he traveled thirty-five miles north to the Colorado border and brought back twenty head of rustled cattle as a wedding present to the sweet Magdalena.

One head at a time, Magda led the cattle to the homes of neighbors who had too many mouths to feed and let them know that the bounty had been provided by her husband. Red rode out again, this time bringing back thirty head. Once again Magda led them away one at a time until there were two left in the pasture owned by her father. This went on until Magda had supplied every family in El Nido with food for the winter and told them that her husband had wanted it so.

It wasn't long before Red realized that he'd married not only a generous woman, but a woman who was determined to make him a hero.

The enemies of El Nido became Red's enemies, and he took seriously his responsibilities as guardian. Neighbors came to the house asking Red to settle disputes with other neighbors. Magda stood behind him reading lips and softly pinching the skin above his belt until he came out with the right answer and everyone went home happy.

Either way, cattle-rustling thief or grandson of a San Patricio, Red's generosity bought the silence of the town. It did no good for the territorial marshal or even the Pinkerton men to come looking for "the murdering, thieving outlaw Booger Red" within his own community. There wasn't a single person who had ever heard of him. The townspeople simply stared at the lawmen and said, "What kind of name is that?" or "You are afraid of a man with such a name?" and laughed out loud until the men with badges turned their horses north and rode off in a cloud of derision toward the Colorado Territory.

Since El Nido now had its own San Patricio (two generations removed), a celebration day was created in Red's honor. It
was held every year somewhere near the time Red had first fallen
off his horse in front of the Sandoval ranch, and every year the
stories of Red's heroism grew until he was both invincible and
sage beyond earthy wisdom. The story was told that Red had
gotten his name because—obviously—he had red hair and had
killed his first man before he was old enough to wipe the snot
from his nose. Of course, each year the number of men Red had
killed before he'd learned to use a handkerchief increased, and
naturally each of these men deserved to die because they had
done some unforgivable mischief to an innocent woman, child,
or dog, and the world was much better off now that Red had
killed the evil person.

In 1914, the same year New Mexico officially joined the
United States, Magda presented Red with a baby boy she named
Rosario De La Cruz Sandoval. The arrival of the little one turned
Red into a doting father whose only desire was to give the two
people in his life as much of the world as he could steal.

One spring Red rode south, telling Magda before he left to
get some men over to till her garden and he'd make it right with
them when he got back. Magda got her garden tilled and waited
twenty-six years for her husband to return.

Every evening she walked the path from her house to
Pump Canyon Road and waited until the sun had gone down.
Neighbors passed and Magdalena waved back to them, but as
soon as they'd gone by, she shaded her eyes against the sun and
resumed searching the road leading south. When Magda wasn't
watching the road, she sat writing things on plain paper. Nobody
knew what she wrote until long after she was dead and one of
the neighbor kids dug his hand down inside a hollowed stump
where Magda used to plant flowers every spring before Booger
left. The boy thought he'd come across a treasure map when he
looked inside the stump and spied chewed edges of brown paper

peeking out from beneath black humus. On each of the pieces of paper Magda had written the date and addressed the pages to "Mi esposo, mi corazón." The letters then went on to tell Red what had happened that day. Each one ended with Magda telling Red that she was sure that a spell had been cast over the house because the rooms had grown too small for her to sit in, and their bed had grown too large for her to lie in.

Magda died at the age of forty-two from a cough brought by the Anglos from the East, never knowing that Red had been hanged in Cottonwood, Arizona, for horse stealing the same spring he left.

A Half Bubble off Plumb

Jimmy De La Cruz thanked the man who'd given him a ride and stepped from the back of the pickup truck to face Our Lady of the Blessed Virgen de Guadalupe. As he crossed the highway and ambled toward the gathering of people, he swiped his hand over his tongue and used the spittle to slick back a few stray hairs.

That morning he had paid a dollar to shower at the Bloomfield truck stop, then dressed himself in the clothes he'd washed two days before at the Sparkle Laundromat. He'd vowed to stay sober throughout the entire celebration of El Día de los Eminentes—a fast of approximately four hours—and left his half-empty quart of Old Grand Dad, along with the rest of his belongings, in the '71 Pontiac where he slept at Montoya's junkyard.

The Day of the Eminent Ones had begun many years before as La Fiesta de los San Patricios, named for Rufus Helmahn Mullerliele, El Nido's first official hero. Although better known throughout the Southwest as Booger Red the Outlaw, within the town of El Nido he was a man known for his wisdom, generosity, and love of community. He was celebrated and his deeds vividly embellished for several decades after his death. But, as with all memories, his legend began to fade. Every year fewer people remembered, until finally the people of El Nido decided it was time to change their celebration of heroes to befit the times. The conclusion of World War II seemed a good time to do this since the town had sacrificed some of its own men for the safety of the world.

The celebration was renamed El Día de los Eminentes and held every year in September. As El Nido's oldest survivor of World War II, Rosario De La Cruz again this year sat at the head of the table at the Guadalupe church picnic. It was common that the appearance of Rosario made strangers turn away, but for the people of El Nido his face held the glory of what they had contributed to the Great War. Thick glasses gave him a cross-eyed look, rather as if he might need help finding his mouth to feed himself. His right cheek was mostly missing, with only shiny, translucent tissue to cover blue veins. The veneer of skin resembled a sheer, dun-colored curtain swept to one side with an invisible clothespin.

Scars ran the length of his arms, and there was a place on his back where the muscle had been spooned out by a bayonet that missed piercing his heart because it bounced off a shoulder blade. Of course the people of El Nido had never seen the hole in his back, and wouldn't have wanted to; the disfigurements on his face and arms were enough to inspire their devotion.

The respect Rosario enjoyed from his neighbors was earned through more than the Great War. He owned his business and established a reputation for honest dealings with customers. If a car didn't need a new fan belt, Rosario did not try to sell a new one while the old one still had some life in it. He trusted people to pay their bills when they said they would, and was more disappointed than angry when they didn't, as if they were children who let him down by failing to keep a cross-your-heart promise. He shared coffee with cronies at the café once in a while on Saturday mornings, but shunned gossip, preferring to discuss the latest equipment on cars, articles in the Albuquerque newspaper, and policies affecting the Veteran's Administration. Rosario held family above all else, forgiving the members of his family for every trespass without their ever asking.

"If a family member steals from you," said Rosario, "you can love him still. Now you know who he is. Or if you give the money, do it knowing it will not come back. What is the worth of a person in your family? I don't know this. But I know that sadness and anger are expensive emotions. They will spend your years two for one." As if setting an insect free, Rosario gave a flip of his hand and advised, "Let it go."

Jimmy lingered at the back of the crowd, self-consciously shaking the hands of people who greeted him. He gazed over the congregation, noting the location of his family, and settled into a chair at one of the farthest tables. He would see his family after the speeches concluded, but right now his head hurt. His hands were shaking, so he kept his arms crossed and his hands tucked under his armpits as if holding his chest muscles against the pull of gravity. If anyone mentioned it, he attributed the perspiration pooling in his pores to the late-summer heat.

Jimmy's grandfather rose from his place at the head table and everyone began to shush the children and settle themselves against the backs of folding chairs. The village of El Nido knew that when Rosario stood up they were about to hear the history of the Bataan Death March. They had heard it many years in a row but it was not a story that tired them. It was a story that made them grateful. Rosario always began with reminding them that 70,000 men—200 times the number of people in El Nido—had been forced to walk sixty-five miles without food or treatment for the wounded. Ten thousand bodies were left along the trail before the march ended, hundreds from infected wounds, thousands from starvation and disease, hundreds more by simply sitting down and deciding to die. Another 6,000, Rosario said, had taken death into their own hands by thinking that an escape into the Philippine jungle offered a chance for survival. At a railhead the men were loaded onto a train bound for a prisoner-of-war camp. Thousands more died at the camp of dysentery, disease, and malnutrition.

Among the ribbons and medals pinned to his jacket, Rosario wore the insignia of the 200th Coast Artillery Regiment, a New Mexico National Guard unit dubbed the "Battling Bastards of Bataan." Only half of the 1,800 Battling Bastards sent to the Philippines survived. Rosario repeated the names of men he had known personally who had died on the infamous march and then, as all survivors do, wondered aloud at why God had spared his life.

When Rosario finished, the people felt wealthy to have beans and tortillas on the table and no sons, brothers, or husbands going off to die, and even the men of El Nido openly wept, Jimmy's tears more forlorn than them all.

Beside Rosario sat Miguel Archunde, El Nido's oldest veteran—indeed, having survived World War I, one of the *world's* oldest veterans. Señor Archunde no longer made speeches or recounted the 1917 trenches of France; his place was to sit as a reminder of El Nido's long history of heroes and sacrifices.

His granddaughter positioned him in a chair and lathered him with praise for sitting quietly, promising him chocolate when the speeches were over. Inevitably though, Señor Archunde began to smile and rock forward and back while repeating, "Buen muchacho. Good boy, good boy."

The congregation indulged him and the speeches proceeded while his granddaughter rushed to give the old man a treat and whisper assurances that everyone thought him a very good boy.

The celebration always included one or two heroes who had done something brave during the previous year. This year Antonio Manzanares shared the head table with Rosario De La Cruz and Señor Archunde. His act of bravery had been to jump into the frozen waters of an inlet of the San Juan River to save his faithful dog from drowning after the animal had broken through a thin mantle of ice.

Antonio listened to praise for his courage, but it brought him little pleasure. Everyone mistook his quiet demeanor for humility, but in reality Antonio was afraid someone in El Nido knew the truth and would stop the ceremony like a jilted lover at a wedding when the preacher asked if there was anyone present who knew why the wedding shouldn't proceed. Antonio was convinced that someone would run from the back of the celebration wagging a finger and shouting that Antonio was a fraud, that he had been frightened the whole time he was rescuing the dog.

The memory of the dog pumping its legs, trying to get a grip on the slosh that kept pulling him deeper, made Antonio squirm in his seat. For Antonio, the recollection of jumping into freezing water felt like one of the biggest mistakes of his life.

As he and the dog suffocated from shock while pounding at slush, digging fingernails and claws into ice that broke apart and disintegrated into the stuff of snow cones, the last thing on Antonio's mind was saving the stupid goddamned dog, and if he could have used the dog's body to save his own, he would have done it. Then, somehow, Antonio had a hold of the dog and they were lying on top of solid ground like two icicles dropped in dirt. For the rest of his life he had no idea how he and the dog had made it out of the water, and back home the two crawled under covers and shook from cold and fear for the next three days.

Antonio now regretted telling his family about the ordeal. The Eminentes celebration was far from his mind when he sat at his mother's kitchen table detailing the calamity that had almost taken his life. His family held their breath at the description of his peril, then applauded the clearheaded actions that resulted in saving himself and his dog. Now he held a plaque and when he stood to deliver a few words to the crowd, he told them honestly that he didn't deserve their admiration.

As with the rest of the crowd, Jimmy De La Cruz sat quietly listening to the account of Antonio's bravery and clapped when the plaque was handed over. But for Jimmy the story was painful. He was filled with jealousy and self-loathing. He listened to his grandfather's story of Bataan, Antonio's story of cheating death, and compared them to the recollection of his own actions in wartime and felt himself compacting into a small box made of shame.

———— • ————

P overty foments barter, and so it was with Genevieve De La Cruz and Lorraine Fay Turnmeyer. In those days the family had no car, which meant that Señor De La Cruz paid another man for a ride to and from his job, and Señora De La Cruz had to strike bargains or ask favors whenever she could to accomplish her own errands. Lorraine Faye Turnmeyer lived in El Nido and worked at a bar in Bloomfield and needed a babysitter for her three-year-old son, Jimmy. Genevieve needed a car once a week to run errands in Farmington. She made a bargain with Lorraine that she would take care of the boy while she worked in exchange for the use of her car for a half day every Monday.

The deal was struck and for two weeks Lorraine Faye picked Jimmy up when she was supposed to, right after her shift at the bar. But then Jimmy's mother began driving up to the house at four in the morning, the car's radio crying its eyes out over drinking alone, cheating hearts, and apologizing to Mama for going to prison, and Lorraine Faye tripping on her own feet as she struggled with the car door. At these times Genevieve stood on the first step of her home, squinting against the car's headlights, her housecoat clutched close at her throat, and calling out to Lorraine that Jimmy should finish staying the night, that it was no trouble, and it being so late . . .

One day, Jimmy's mother dropped him off with more clothing than she usually brought. With little more than a wave, she never returned. Genevieve did not notify the authorities that she was harboring a child who was missing a mother; she added more beans to the pot, crowded another pallet into the room where her other five children slept, and neatly patched the hand-me-down clothing from her older boys.

She treated Jimmy as one of her own, tending his cuts and bruises when he was hurt and making sure he was given the same portions at mealtime as the other children. She spoke to him in Spanish until he understood and spoke it back to her. Jimmy's new siblings laughed at his Spanish, and once Genevieve overheard the mimicry, she would have none of it. She sent her husband and little Jimmy outside to pick tomatoes from the garden, then sat her other children down and explained to them that Jimmy's speech impediment was not to be ridiculed in any language.

For several years after his mother disappeared, Jimmy held onto a fold of Genevieve's skirt. He grew adept at whirling around the kitchen as Genevieve moved from stove to sink, from cupboard to counter. If Genevieve needed him out of the way, she plopped him atop a stool, where he sat silently pulling on an earlobe and looking at the world with patient eyes while Genevieve mixed flour and lard, salt and baking soda, then tepid water to make the masa for tortillas.

His brothers and sisters included him in their play, protected him at school when the other children made fun of the way he talked, and lied for him just as they did for each other when he did something mischievous. Señor De La Cruz threw the same number of pitches to him as he did his other sons, taught him the same chores, and disciplined him no more and no less than the other children.

Everyone in El Nido knew that little Jimmy had been left behind by a mother whose whereabouts remained unknown, but no one at the school asked for adoption papers when Genevieve signed him up for kindergarten as Santiago De La Cruz. Throughout his school years when Jimmy had to fill out forms asking his ancestry, he invariably marked "Hispanic." No one at the school ever corrected him or re-marked the form.

Eventually, Sheriff Max got a teletype saying a woman named Lorraine Faye Turnmeyer had been found dead from an alcohol overdose in a Durango motel room. He drove to El Nido to deliver the news that Lorraine Faye would never return for her son. Genevieve made the sign of the cross, uttering, "Qué desgracia." Within herself, however, she breathed, "Gracias a Dios."

When the Vietnam war came, Jimmy was the only one from the De La Cruz family who was the right age and in the right situation for the government to want him. He'd graduated from high school and worked for his grandfather Rosario at the garage on the corner of First and Main in Bloomfield for a year or so when the draft notice came in the mail in May of 1971. There was no such thing as burning draft cards in El Nido; the young men who were called went without thought or complaint, although their mothers thought and complained about it a great deal. Genevieve appealed to Jimmy's high school English teacher to write to the draft board and explain that Jimmy should be dismissed from duty since he had a speech impediment that might make it difficult for people to understand him, and wouldn't that be dangerous in time of war? The army never wrote back and Jimmy boarded a bus on the designated day.

At three in the morning on the day he was to leave for Vietnam, Jimmy crept into the family kitchen to find the only man he'd known as a father sitting at the table. They made hot chocolate together instead of coffee, believing they might be able to sleep again, then settled into chairs as Jimmy's father said, "Three o'clock is always too late or too early for anything you want to do, ¿que no?" Father and son laughed in agreement and took turns listing all the things they could not do at three in the morning. "Da bars are cwosed," said Jimmy. "The newspaper hasn't come," said Alfredo. "Ya can't caw anyone 'less der's been a deaf in da fam'ly," said Jimmy. "And your wife will protest if you wake her," his father said with a chuckle.

In spite of it all, said Jimmy's father, he was always happy to wake up at three in the morning because at his age it meant he was still alive. He told Jimmy he'd read somewhere that three o'clock was the dying hour. Science had proved it. The article said that the heart slows down, even stops for a split second to take a rest around that time, and if a person was already in poor health, well, perhaps they couldn't spare that one skipped beat.

Jimmy nodded his head as if he understood the fears of advancing middle age, then the two men sat in silence, staring into the cups as if chocolate dregs had the same power to foretell the future as tea leaves.

"Are you afraid, son?" Alfredo De La Cruz asked at last.

"No, Dad," said Jimmy, smiling at his father, "Ahm ten foot taw and bulwet-pwoof."

The day before Jimmy became a coward, he and the four men left in his unit walked through a village they would have sworn they'd seen before: a lot of women and children and old men, a place to fill canteens, a chance to perhaps pilfer some food. The villagers tried not to look at the soldiers walking among them, and those who did look were men bowing deeply, smiling, hoping their humility might keep everyone alive. The people went about their work, the routine they'd set for themselves, the things that helped them hold onto a world without destroyed crops and dead relatives.

A woman in the village reminded Jimmy of his mother. The woman looked near his mother's age and had the same small, strong hands, with work-dried, flaky skin in the cracks of her knuckles. She had the middle-aged round belly of his mother and the assiduous eyes of a woman who does not believe in idle time. She had just washed her hair and now left it hanging down past her hips to dry in the sun. It was the one thing about the woman that still resembled youth. Watching the hair swirl from side to side as she bent over her work, Jimmy wanted to move close to her. He wanted to smell her hair.

When he was a boy he felt the safest, the most serene when his mother took him on her lap to tell him a story and check the cleanliness of his ears. It was at those times that Genevieve took the pins from her hair and let it fall in spirals around her shoulders and down to her waist. When the storytelling ended and his mother pronounced him clean, she often leaned over to kiss his belly or bury her face in his neck to tickle him and Jimmy smelled the hair as it swirled like dark silk around his whole small body.

Jimmy knew that if he wanted to go up to the woman and smell her hair, there would be nothing anyone could do about it. Soldiers were always accommodated in the villages. People were held prisoner by both sides due to the inherent helplessness of civilians in a war zone. But Jimmy did not go to the woman demanding that she render him an echo of his childhood. He thought of his own

mother and imagined her fear if a soldier came to her house and
then wanted to come close to her. The thought of someone making
his mother afraid angered him, made him feel the focused vicious-
ness of an animal protecting his clan. He banished his need to stand
near to the woman and simply drew in a breath through his nostrils
and sniffed the scent of soap that wasn't there at all.

Jimmy knew he was a coward. His moments of longing for
home, of not understanding the war were not moments at all. They
were not private instances of pondering human motivation or the
reasons for war or his place on the stage of human drama. They
were moments strung together without spaces of aching to be in
his mother's kitchen, to be working in his grandfather's garage, to
be surrounded by Spanish-speaking people who shared his very
same life.

Jimmy knew he lived in a democracy because that was what
he'd been told in high school, but that was the extent of what he
knew about protecting Vietnam against communism. He had no
understanding of how life would be different for the Vietnamese
if they were Democrats or Republicans or communists, and he didn't
understand how he was making a difference.

He had no stomach for it, and the knowledge made him
ashamed. He knew that when he shot back at objects, it was terror that moved him to action. His shots were often wild, with his
bullets ending up embedded in trees. He shot low, avoiding kill
shots to the head or abdomen. When it was over, he shook inside
his clothing, refusing to speak for hours after skirmishes, sucking
on the insides of his cheeks to keep down the bile that raced up
and down his throat.

He knew that the men in his unit knew he was a coward. They
knew he shook. They knew he was the last to return fire when
something started, as if he had to be convinced every single time
that this was real and there was no option but to shoot back.

The soldiers left the village after a perfunctory search of rice
barrels and huts and walked toward a rendezvous with another

unit. Into the late afternoon sun the march became haphazard, the men less attentive than they should have been. They knew better. They knew that when they rocked themselves to sleep with the rhythm of their own powdered footsteps in the dirt, when they dozed on their feet with thoughts of a girlfriend's smooth skin, the smell of a mother's freshly cooked food, or of conspiring with a best friend to pull off a high school prank, that those were the most dangerous times.

Had there been a neutral observer, it would have been difficult to decide which group of men was the more startled when five Americans and a handful of Vietcong were suddenly standing less than twelve yards apart. The Americans fell to the ground, hoping to make themselves flat, and they were the first to pull off rounds as the Vietcong flew toward the cover of trees and tall bushes. One of the Vietnamese did a sort of graceful leap, then plummeted to the ground as if suddenly erased from the landscape by a dissatis- fied artist. The rest of the Vietcong disappeared into trees and jungle grass while the American soldiers squinted against the sun for signs of hiding places betrayed by rustling leaves.

There was nowhere to go, so the men began pushing them- selves backward like skittish lizards trying to fit under a low rock. Their elbows akimbo, and their legs splayed out as if their thigh muscles had been cut, the men couldn't see where they were going. They only knew they must put some distance, some camouflage between themselves and the men who had access to trees. They kept up their backward slither until they felt the ground beneath them give way. A shelf of land tapered off, giving them a four-foot drop to safety.

"So this is home," said Private Matthews, a man who had become Jimmy's friend since they'd been assigned to the same unit.

"What now?" said another man.

"We wait," answered Trigger, the unit's leader.

As much as the men despised him, they knew that Trigger was right. There was nothing to do but wait. The other unit would be coming soon. They had orders to join them and they couldn't let them walk into an ambush.

The body of the Vietnamese soldier lay halfway between the American soldiers and the Vietcong. The Vietcong would not leave without the body of their comrade and the Americans couldn't leave without warning the forthcoming unit. They also couldn't allow the Vietcong to calmly walk into the clearing between them and retrieve the body without shooting at the enemy.

The two sides settled in for a night of waiting, listening. Now it began—the incident that removed all doubt that Jimmy De La Cruz was indeed a coward.

⁂

P ssst, Jimbo, my turn yet?" Private Matthews's voice came from among a huddle of bodies.

"Go bac' ta sweep," said Jimmy, looking at his watch. "Not you turn 'til five."

"Can't sleep any more anyway."

Jimmy watched Matthews unwind himself from the sleeping men. They lay together in a crook of the shelf looking like the bodies of dead men put to one side after a battle and Jimmy had to remind himself that they were only sleeping. The men gave a stretch to locked bones and compressed muscles. They yawned without sound and blinked like children who'd been moved from their beds and were waking up in a strange house, then the men filled the spot left by Matthews and returned to sleep.

"What the hell happened to the other unit?" Matthews wondered without expecting an accurate answer.

Jimmy whispered a perfunctory "Doe know," and the silence closed around them for another moment.

"Anything happening over there?" asked Matthews.

"Noffing's happuned since dis stwarted," said Jimmy.

"Is the body even still there? Maybe they got the body and left."

"I's stil' der," said Jimmy.

"What do you think they're up to?"

"I tink der jus' wike us," said Jimmy. "I tink der tiwred and hungwee. I tink dey ain't goin' widout da body."

"Well, they ain't like us," hissed a voice from the darkness. "They ain't like us at all. They're gooks, and something is gonna happen real soon even if I gotta make it happen. I gar-run-damn-tee ya."

Like a needle poking into flesh, the voice coming out of the darkness was Trigger. It wasn't his real name, of course, but the men dubbed him this because he never had his finger off the trigger of his gun. Most of the men refused to walk ahead of him because of this habit, anxious that the finger always stood too much at the ready, and they were convinced that he'd shoot one of them in the back one day. Trigger made no protest about this. He liked being point man and taunted his fellow soldiers with lowbred names for women's private areas when they spoke of the danger.

Trigger wormed his way to where Jimmy and Matthews lay peering into the darkness.

"Can you still see the body?" asked Trigger as he adjusted himself near the men.

"Yeah, it's there," said Matthews.

All three men focused until they could see the outline of the dead Vietnamese man lying halfway between themselves and where they knew the Vietcong were stationed in trees and tall grass.

"You know they ain't gonna leave without him," said Trigger. "Which means none of us is leaving here until one side kills the other."

The men lay quietly on their bellies, watching the outline of the body.

"I say we go get the body," said Trigger.

"What the hell for?" snapped Matthews.

"To force 'em into something. All we're doing is sitting here— *been* sitting here for hours. And besides, the dead guy's got ammo."

"Das sulcide, Twigger," said Jimmy.

"Yeah, you're nuttier than I thought you were," said Matthews.

"You're a bunch of pansies. I'm going. You guys just cover me in case the gooks are up watching the late show," Trigger replied.

"Doe't do ot, Twigger, we doe't even know whear dey are," said Jimmy, pulling at Trigger's sleeve.

Trigger jerked his arm from Jimmy's grip. "I'm going," he said, and he began snaking his way through the grass toward the body. He did it so silently that at first Jimmy and Matthews thought he wasn't moving at all. But then, as the two watched, the silhouette of the dead body in the distance suddenly came alive. As if resurrected, the body moved its arms, raised its head just slightly. The Vietcong finally saw it too and the darkness became a backdrop for the fire spitting out of automatic weapons.

Jimmy and Matthews returned the volley, unable to see what they were shooting at but keeping their guns raised away from where they knew Trigger and the body were entangled. The sleeping men jumped to help, blasting treetops with bullets.

When Trigger first got to the body, he thought the job would be easy. It looked as if the ammunition pack would slide straight away from the dead man's shoulder with just a tug. But the pack got hung up on an elbow in rigor mortis and Trigger had to raise himself a bit to get a grip on the pack, had to raise the dead man's arm to untangle the strap, and that's when the shooting began. Trigger pulled the dead man on top of himself and began moving back toward his men, using the body as a shield. He could feel that the body had been hit several times before he reached Jimmy and Matthews, could feel the wetness of body fluid trickle into his clothing. His nostrils were full of the body's stench and now he would be wearing the body's blood and ooze on his own body.

Trigger got the body back to the men and in a few minutes the shooting subsided.

"Now you've done it," hissed Matthews. "Now you've done it, you stupid mother . . . " Jimmy sat wide-eyed looking at Trigger, looking at the body.

"That's right, asshole, now it's done," spit Trigger.

The first hint of daylight had shone itself during the foray and now the men could better see the object that had kept them all waiting to move on. They could see the wound that had killed the dead man because that one was crusted over near the heart. The bullet wounds he had sustained while saving the life of Trigger did not ooze regular blood, but rather various sorts of liquid, watery pink in one place, yellow-white syrup in another, dark purple the viscosity of thickened pudding in another. The dark purple reminded Jimmy of the blood pudding the old women from El Nido made after slaughtering a lamb. Jimmy had never had a taste for blood pudding.

All the men stood staring at the body. It was bloated to twice the size of the man who had once lived inside it. The face looked like a cartoon character who'd been hit with a frying pan; the body itself resembled an effigy stuffed with straw. Next to the man lay a small mélange of possessions. As Trigger had pulled him down the draw, the man's pockets had emptied and the contents lay in a line along the drag marks. Instead of a wallet, the man carried a pouch drawn together with leather strings. The strings had come loose and now the things it once harbored lay beside him. Jimmy was the first to notice the contents of the man's pockets spilling out onto the earth. There were coins and piasters of several denominations and the men standing around the body recognized that they had used this same money in Hanoi bars and other places much safer than where they now stood.

"His stuff," said Jimmy, making a move toward the body, then pulling back.

The men had been told that communists were godless, and yet, there lay Jesus stretched across the face of a cross and— although he didn't formulate the impression in linear thought—it struck Jimmy as odd that this man carried for the same reason the same symbol of the same God his mother assured him would save his life. Next to the coins and under the cross lay pictures. Jimmy picked these up and blew away dirt with a quick puff.

One of the pictures showed a family gathered at some sort of celebration. Jimmy could tell it was a celebration because a lot of people were sitting at a table laden with food. The women wore bright-colored silks and had decorations in their hair. Next to one woman sat a man Jimmy thought might be the dead man. Next to them sat an old couple, smiling slightly with arms interlocked. It was an anniversary party, thought Jimmy. The old couple were the dead man's parents. Yes, that's what it was. Or perhaps a birthday party for one of the man's parents.

Jimmy moved closer and stared into another picture of the same woman, who was sitting next to the dead man in the celebration picture. Again she wore trinkets in her hair. Her smile was slight, more as if she was looking at the person who was looking at her, as if the paper she was printed on was a window and Jimmy was a benign voyeur who'd been caught.

The other men seemed more mesmerized by the body itself, the fluid sieving out of the openings, the stench of the decay, the disbelieving hypnosis of death. Jimmy broke the trance by leaning down to the man and picking up the last of his belongings. He gathered the things that belonged in the pouch and put them back inside. Then he kneaded the pouch into the man's pocket.

"I wanna give 'em bac'," said Jimmy. The men thought Jimmy meant he wanted to do just what he had already done—give back to the dead man his possessions. They stood mute while Jimmy went beyond putting the belongings into pockets and began straightening the man's shirt and smoothing down his hair. They watched without comprehension when Jimmy picked up a rag Trigger had discarded after wiping down his rifle and began tying it to the muzzle of his own rifle. The men watched the fingers tie the knot, watched the hands raise the barrel above Jimmy's head, watched the oily, soot-streaked flag flutter like a molting bird tethered to a pole against its will. Then they watched as Jimmy took the dead man by the back of the collar and began pulling him up the incline. They were so hypnotized by the flutter of the flag and the tracks left by the pull of the dead man's body that they did not try to stop him, nor were they able to give warning before Trigger came from behind and smashed the butt of his rifle between Jimmy's shoulders.

"What do you think you're doing!" screamed Trigger. "You coward, you goddamned nutcase sissy coward!" Jimmy did not stay down; it seemed as if the blow barely caught his attention. Instead, he grabbed at dirt, trying to pull himself along while still holding on to the rifle flying the dingy rag and the scruff of the dead man's collar. Without looking at Trigger, he said only, "Ahm goin' home."

"I'll shoot you myself, you hear me? I'll shoot you myself!" Trigger shouldered his rifle.

"Eeveer way," said Jimmy without looking at Trigger, "ahm goin' home."

Shouldering his rifle was the last thing Trigger did before he saw scores of pinpoint diamonds hurtling into the black velvet of an abyss. Matthews stood over him poised to deliver another blow if needed. But it was not needed, and the diamonds traveled at the speed of light until they disappeared and Trigger slept, enveloped in the black velvet long enough for yet another man to save his life that day.

Matthews watched Jimmy's silhouette pull itself upright against the dim light of morning. The gun with the flag fell to the ground and the silhouette pulled the dead man's body behind it. Then Matthews heard the silhouette calling out to the trees, to the grass, to the sound of breathing where no faces could be seen.

"Hey, ya guys," called Jimmy, "Heaw's you buddy. We dent take none o' his stuff." Jimmy reached for something in back of himself and Matthews was sure the move would provoke a volley of fire. But no shots came from the trees, no sound, no movement.

"Hey, ya guys," called Jimmy to the phantoms, "I wanna go home." He held his wallet up near his cheek and let the flap of pictures fold out of the wallet. "Thees are my paywents. Dey lub me."

Jimmy continued to walk forward in a simple saunter that might have made him look like a small boy preoccupied with kicking leaves except for the body he dragged along behind him.

"An' thees is my sistor. Anna. She da smart one. She goin' ta cawedge."

Jimmy tripped over vines but righted himself without going down. "Thees my brudder, Alfaydo. He was named fo' my dad." Jimmy stopped midway between where the Vietnamese men were hiding in the jungle and where his own men huddled in the draw. Jimmy couldn't see the Vietcong, but he knew the men were there; he thought he could hear them blinking their eyes.

"Thees is my mom." Jimmy looked at the picture, then held it out again. "She allays kweening sumfing," Jimmy said. "Allays cooking sumfing."

Jimmy let go of the body and let it fall gently into the grass.

"Ahm goin' home," said Jimmy.

First a rustle to Jimmy's left, then another to his right, and then way up in the trees the leaves fluttered. Jimmy watched the flutters and rustles then heard nothing at all, not even the sound of breathing.

"OK," said Jimmy, turning around to walk back toward his friends. "OK."

Jimmy walked away with his back to the phantoms in the trees. He felt as if he had a hangover: thickheaded, sick to his stomach, his body the weight of a monument. He walked toward the men with whom he had shared youth. He saw on their faces a disbelief and a relief that the standoff was over. But he missed the look of admiration behind their eyes. He missed it altogether as he walked slump-shouldered and weary back to where Trigger still lay in the land of stars while the other men stood in a land of morbid reality, never questioning until that moment why they had agreed to kill people they would have never otherwise met on the streets of home.

Trigger awoke spitting threats of court martial until Matthews reminded him that it was a long way back to base. Anything could happen between here and there, Matthews said. Life being as risky as it was in wartime, Trigger could get shot before they made it back to the platoon. Snipers can take the back of your head off just like that—and the mother-jumpers are everywhere, said Matthews. Perhaps Trigger wasn't remembering right about what happened just before he lost consciousness. Perhaps he should leave the telling of the story—if there was a story to tell at all—to the other men, since he was out cold from hitting his head when he fainted.

J immy waited for the speeches to end, knowing he could slip away when people got up to fill their plates. At the El Nido Highway he put out his thumb and as he walked backward he assured himself that he would see his family some other time. He renewed his daily vow that tomorrow would be the first day of a sober life. He would finish that one bottle left in the car at the junkyard and tomorrow he would ask someone for a ride to an AA meeting. Or maybe he'd go all the way and call the Veteran's Administration. He'd ask his brother to loan him the money for a ticket to Albuquerque, where the VA had the rehab. He'd pay his brother back as soon as his disability check came at the first of the month.

Yes, tomorrow for sure.

Or he could wait until the first of the month and buy his own bus ticket and no one would have to know he'd gone into rehab. And then he would surprise everyone and show up on his parents' doorstep after thirty days sober and they'd be happy to see him and his mother wouldn't look at him so sadly anymore. Maybe he could hold a job. Get a car. Have his own apartment in Farmington.

It was settled: the first of the month for sure.

Jimmy's mother watched her son disappear into the crowd and reappear on the highway. She knew, the family knew, about the bottles, the countless bottles, since returning from Vietnam. They knew that Jimmy had become someone the town called Bubbles because, they said, he was a half bubble off plumb. A little crazy, they said when they happened to see him walking along the roads, but harmless.

A Believable Story

I t's a heavy burden knowing your mother is a liar. Not just a harmless fibber or entertaining embellisher, but a liar. The sort of liar that when someone earnestly inquires how your mother is recuperating from a political madman's attack while she was in Brazil ministering to the poor, the only thing to do is stand perfectly still, mouth agape, eyes blinking in rhythm with the brain as it ticks off the list of available answers. And when asked what is the matter, the only retort can be a babble that the whole thing is too difficult to talk about—but you certainly appreciate the concern.

What else is there to say? It's your mother, for God's sake, and exposing her for what she is would be more embarrassing than hearing the lie. It would also be treason. You can't go around letting others know your mother is a liar. Elvira's mother would never forgive her—if she knew her daughter knew.

Elvira's mother is a good liar: adept, convincing, and benign in intent. Now, theoretically, it is *possible*—on some planet in the universe, perhaps one without gravity—that Elvira's mother actually did survive a plane crash over the Atlantic and swim out to save a small child, grabbing the cords of the child's life jacket between her teeth and pulling the helpless thing back to the fold of the surviving group huddled on the floating wing of the broken airplane. The story continues that credit must be given to the other survivors for their encouragement while Elvira's mother sustained the child with mouth-to-mouth for several hours until the rescue team came.

Then, of course, she bravely stayed behind until all were pulled to safety ahead of her.

Elvira wanted to believe her mother was a heroine in a world of ordinary people, and she knew her mother as a wonderfully kind woman—but she can't swim.

Elvira's mother is a believable liar because she's laid the foundation for credibility in the way she conducts the rest of her life. She's an honest, hardworking, sincerely compassionate woman, so it's impossible for the people listening to the lies to believe she's lying. It's true—the part about being honest, hardworking, and sincere. Elvira's mother would walk a mile to return an overpaid nickel, and stories of treachery or discord between partners, friends, or family send her into a spell of tongue-clucking and prayers to God to send peace and wisdom to the people involved.

She is a smart liar because she tells much smaller lies within the boundaries of El Nido. These lies pass with little notice because it's in the nature of Hispanic people to be tolerant, even supportive, of exaggeration, minor mischief, and benign delusion, especially in family members. Elvira once consulted her tía Salina, a nurse at San Juan Hospital, about her mother's lies, hoping her aunt might intervene in some way. But her aunt knew only of the small lies her sister told and advised Elvira to be tolerant of her mother's peculiarities because, Dios sabe, there was much worse deception perpetrated on society every day of the week than that of a middle-aged woman exaggerating a bruised toe into a broken foot.

Elvira could not bring herself to divulge her mother's big lies in order to convince her aunt that her mother's stories were more serious than hypochondria, so she kissed Tía Salina's cheek and returned home feeling more alone than ever.

Elvira's mother tells her lies only to people who live out of town. These anxious out-of-towners call Elvira to ask how her mother is doing because they don't want to disturb her so soon after the kidnapping. They don't mean to pry, and they apologize for making Elvira relive the anguish, but they simply must know how the lesions from the abductors' whips are healing. And, by the way, has she heard anything from the Mexican police about making an arrest?

Usually, when these distressed friends call, the first thing Elvira says is notably awkward and inappropriate, like, "Hold on, the kids have the TV blaring and I can't hear a thing." Elvira then paces the floor for a moment or two mumbling, "Kidnapping, kidnapping." Returning to the phone, she might ask, "Now what were you saying?" And they commence again, with no less fervor in their voices than when Elvira had first answered the phone.

"Elvira," they say, "we are absolutely devastated to hear of your mother's terrible experience."

Elvira assures them that she too is devastated.

She has found that the best way to handle these heartfelt inquiries is with assurances of her mother's astounding energy for life and it's-the-will-of-God-type clichés.

Elvira's mother is a convincing liar because she makes sure there is only one lie per acquaintance. She seems to know quite instinctively that, even with her well-established credibility, a plane crash and a kidnapping in one lifetime is stretching the inherent gullibility of friendship beyond its limits. The Alcóns from Albuquerque get the plane crash; the Madrids, retired in El Paso, get the madman attack; and the Tafoyas, residing in Chimayó, get the near-death experience with comprehensive details; such as the brilliant white light, the celestial music, and the ancestors waiting with arms unfurled to welcome her into the kingdom of heaven—although, gracias a Dios, her grandmother showed up in the nick of time to say she wasn't supposed to be dead yet and sent her back, mentioning just as Elvira's mother exited backward through the white-light portal that there was a lot of work to be done among the poor in Brazil.

Each in turn, these people have hung up the phone satisfied that Elvira's high-spirited mother is recovering as well as can be expected in the loving company of her daughter. Elvira, on the other hand, hangs up the phone and begins to clean house. She can't help it. After one of her mother's stories she must clean something, straighten things, remove junk from overstuffed drawers, coordinate her clothes closet by season and fabric content.

But this time her mother's lies promise grave consequences. This time it's serious, very serious, and cleaning house is not going to save her mother's life.

Elvira's mother, a widow, bears a striking resemblance to her daughter and looks younger than her real age. The two are often mistaken for sisters when they stroll through shops. (In spite of this, Elvira's mother also lies about her age, making herself older so people will be even more amazed at her youthful appearance.) Her shiny dark hair is barely streaked with gray, and, like so many Hispanic women, Elvira's mother has not cut her hair simply because she's aging. She still wears it past her shoulders, often pinning it up to frame high cheekbones and red lips. Her face carries only soft creases, the sort of lines that most people would say do not connote age but serve to trace the sparkle of her smile, and she doesn't weigh an ounce more than she did the day she graduated from high school.

It's small wonder then that gentlemen of accomplishment and consequence seek her company—and that is where it got serious.

One of these gentlemen is retired air force Colonel Harold Brubaker, and he is a man who enjoys jumping out of airplanes—skydiving. It was a most unfortunate thing that he was the one Elvira's mother had chosen to tell that she was the first woman in New Mexico to successfully parachute to the ground with her Chihuahua, Pedro, strapped to her chest. She considered herself rather like the woman who went over Niagara Falls nailed inside a barrel while holding onto her cat.

Elvira's mother had explained that of course the dog was never quite the same afterward, and never jumped up onto so much as a chair again for the rest of its life, but sharing the experience with her loving companion was more than she could resist.

Upon hearing this story, Colonel Brubaker was elated. He immediately had visions of himself and Elvira's mother descending hand in hand through 13,000 feet of clouds and no oxygen to the scenic valley floor, then enjoying a catered candlelight dinner at the hangar while still wearing matching flight suits.

It was to be a surprise.

He had called the Wednesday before to enlist Elvira's assistance, telling her to fabricate a need for her mother to join her on an errand and then actually deliver her to Sky Park. He would have everything ready at his end, he said.

Elvira heard him out and felt her breathing become labored. She began straightening her children's homework on the dining room table. Before she could stop herself, she erased the answers in her son's workbook and rewrote them more neatly. While holding the phone in one hand, Elvira dampened a paper towel and stood in the middle of her kitchen desperately looking for a corner to clean. What was she to do? She couldn't hand her mother over to certain death, and she couldn't betray her mother by telling Brubaker the truth. She did the only thing a person in her position could do: She lied.

"This is out of the question, Colonel Brubaker," Elvira said, "Mother had back surgery not long ago and . . ."

Nonsense, he replied, the accident resulting from the women's toboggan competition was ten years ago. Surely she was fully recovered by now. Was Elvira blind?

"She walks with the gait of a thirty-year-old and the exuberance of a teenager. A most exciting woman," Brubaker said.

He would have none of Elvira's excuses. She was being overprotective and, he suspected, a bit jealous. He assured her that another man would soon come into her life, a better one than her ex-husband, who had abandoned his family for drink, younger women, and life on an oil rig off the Pacific coast of Mexico.

Elvira pictured her ex-husband puttering in his kitchen, attired in an apron with a naked Adonis printed on the front while making dinner for his lover, Royce, and groaned.

The conversation ended with Colonel Brubaker instructing Elvira to transport her mother to hangar B on Saturday afternoon at three o'clock sharp. She hung up the phone and slumped against the breakfast bar. Hangar B. Bloody begins with the letter B. Broken bones. Blackened. Burned. (Do bodies combust upon impact?) For "blat" (which is the sound her mother would make just as she hits the ground) for blasphemous (which is the kind of sound Elvira will make after her mother hits the ground). Dear God, B is for bereaved. It was, as they say, an omen.

In retrospect, Elvira believed there was more she could have done, questions she should have demanded answers to, action she should have taken. She thought back now and speculated that surely there must have been something she could have done sooner to relieve her torment. Instead, she allowed her anguish to consume and paralyze her, render her incapable of logical thought and purposeful action.

She considered telling Colonel Brubaker that her mother was a woman given to grandiose prevarications fomented by a profound need for self-aggrandizement—in short, a compulsive liar—but in the end she couldn't do it.

She pondered a confrontation with her mother, blurting out that she knew everything, while assuring her that she still thought her a stellar woman, and this one flaw in her character in no way diminished her love for her. Perhaps, she had meant to say, this affliction is treatable. She would have declared that her only concern was that her mother save her own life.

Elvira remained a coward, incapable of watching her mother turn crimson with embarrassment—or worse, deny all. It terrified Elvira that her mother might lie and then swear to actually having done the things she lied about doing. She might go on to calmly explain that she kept the kidnapping from Elvira in order to save her the worry, that the plane crash rescue had been what any compassionate human being would have done and there was no need for applause. She might say the Madrids had somehow misunderstood the purpose of the vacation she took to Brazil some years ago; the women's toboggan competition and parachuting were merely hobbies, hardly worth mentioning.

But now, Elvira would never know what her mother might have said; the time for questions had passed.

When the women arrived at Sky Park, Elvira's mother was delighted to see Colonel Brubaker holding flowers and waving for them to hurry. Elvira had driven slowly into Farmington, making them late, hoping Brubaker's masculine imagination would assume himself to be stood up and leave without her mother.

Two hangar attendants flanked Brubaker on either side and smiled broadly. Their smiles reminded Elvira of ghouls stimulated by the sight of a fresh corpse. Brubaker walked briskly to the passenger side of the car and quickly whisked Elvira's mother into the hangar where he and the two attendants began ritually dressing her in a flight suit too closely resembling a preliminary body bag. He disclosed his lovely surprise to Elvira's mother while cinching up belts and adjusting zippers, but it was Elvira who received the shock. She had expected her mother's face to crumble; she strained her eyes for some sign of trepidation, a grasping for an excuse not to go. Instead, her mother seemed jubilant, eager to fulfill her destiny. Elvira could take no more.

It was one long scream at first, the sort of scream that rivets an audience more on the screamer than on the cause. Then the scream metamorphosed into babble.

"Dile, Mamá. Dile que no puedes. Tell him you can't do this. Please, Mother, don't go."

"There, there," said Elvira's mother, "not a thing to worry about, mijita. Colonel Brubaker will take good care of me, won't you, Harold?"

Elvira's mother is patting the top of her daughter's head because her daughter has dropped to her knees and is screaming as she buries her face into her mother's stomach, her arms clenched around the top of her mother's thighs.

Colonel Brubaker is trying to pry Elvira's arms loose so he can finish hooking up her mother's gear. "Elvira," says Brubaker, "I have a son. I'll introduce you to him. You'll forget all about the brute who left you."

"He makes quiche!" shrieks Elvira.

What? What is she saying, they ask each other. The two mechanics stand frozen, confused at the scene before them.

Did they really believe Elvira would give her mother over without a fight?

"Adonis . . . naked . . . apron," Elvira blithers. Then, deciding it's time for determined words, she musters a threat. "I'll tell him if you don't. I will. Don't make me do it. Por favor, Madre, I am begging you."

Elvira's mother continues to pat her daughter's head while the exasperated Colonel Brubaker momentarily gives up on pulling at arms and stands away in disgust.

"She had a very high fever when she was a small child," says Elvira's mother, as if her daughter is not there. "Gets high-strung once in a while ever since."

"Should we call 911?" asks Brubaker.

"Oh, no," says the mother gently. "It's just one of her little fits. She'll be fine soon."

Brubaker looks unconvinced. "I don't know how you put up with this," he says, shaking his head and walking away to stand in a huddle with the hangar attendants.

What was she thinking, Elvira says to herself. I'm bigger than she is; three inches taller and twenty pounds stronger. I'll just drag her out of here.

Her sobs turn to hiccups as she pivots her face toward the opening of the hangar to assess the distance. It's not that far; I could easily pull her to the car before anyone would be able to stop us.

The grip on her mother's thighs has relaxed while Elvira decides where to grab her mother next.

"That's a good girl. Yes, let Mother go."

Elvira decides to reason with her mother one more time before dragging her away.

"Mother, you can't do this. Tell him anything. For God's sake, *liiiiiie!*"

Jerking her head up as if suddenly touched with the gift of prophecy, Elvira stares into her mother's face with narrowed eyes. "Let's kill him. If we kill him, no one will ever know you didn't go."

The next thing Elvira knows, two men have come from behind, each of them taking an arm, and they begin lugging her backward. These are the same two men, she's sure, who will be the first to find the splattered remains of her mother's body and she will be right behind them shouting I-told-you-sos and flailing them across their backs like a medieval executioner with whatever is handy.

Colonel Brubaker runs alongside the ridiculous procession, telling Elvira in a soothing voice about his son, the one who's making a mint with his successful interior design business in San Francisco. A family man with no aversion to helping in the kitchen. Indeed, after thirty-five years of bachelorhood the son is quite a cook—and very tidy. Just a little shy around women— hasn't met the right one yet.

"Don't hurt her," calls Elvira's mother as the men haul her farther away from her mother. The mother's arms are stretched forward like a clumsy kindergartner attempting to catch a ball. Brubaker returns and takes Elvira's mother by the elbow, guiding her toward the airplane, its engine already revved. Elvira's mother looks back over her shoulder several times, sending what are meant to be comforting but nonetheless worried smiles. Elvira continues shrieking and furiously undulating her body against the two men until she sees her mother and Brubaker step inside the belly of the plane and the door close behind them.

Then the struggle is over. The two hangar attendants are left holding a mere apparition of the woman who, just moments before, fought so valiantly to save her mother's life. They slacken their grip and pilot her toward a chair, propping her into it like a cloth doll, and stand away to discuss what should be done with her. While stroking his chin and sneaking surreptitious glances, the taller of the two men mentions coffee. He ponders that Elvira might be more comfortable lying down on the cot usually reserved for late-working mechanics. The other man has had enough of Elvira and suggests tethering her to the chair, but the chin-stroker will have none of it and refuses to help. Neither one of them realizes that as soon as Elvira sees her mother's remains she will murder them both.

The tall chin-stroker finally dismisses the other man and approaches Elvira, carrying a steaming cup of coffee. Positioning a chair next to Elvira, he quietly asks if she wants the cup. She takes it from him without gratitude and uses it only to warm her hands, which feel bloodless and shaky.

"Your mother is going to be fine," he says gently. Elvira stares at him as if he's out of focus and says nothing. He shifts in his chair. "Why are you so nervous? Why is this time any different than the others?" he asks softly, as if he is genuinely interested in hearing an explanation.

Others? His face comes into focus and Elvira sees that his eyes are the color of green peridot. The lashes are dark brown, almost black, like his hair. The chin he is so fond of caressing is sturdy yet pliant, and his mouth turns upward at the edges.

"What others?" says Elvira. The coffee cup has become a giant rosary bead.

"The other times your mother has gone skydiving."

"But she hasn't!" Elvira's voice is shrill again and the man pulls back.

"Of course she has," says the man kindly. His chin offers him no comfort; his hands fly slightly open, away from his body, the fingers splayed in a gesture of sympathetic but worn-thin patience.

"We can't allow people to just show up and jump out of airplanes. They have to be certified."

Did he say certified or certifiable?

"Certified?" The word rolled in her mouth like a piece of food foreign to her palate.

"Your mother has to have a license. She has to have one before we let her on the plane."

"Did you see the license? Did she show you a license?"

The man thought for a second, then said, "But Brubaker, he arranged everything. Surely he would know . . . he said she wouldn't have it with her because of the surprise."

The man looks worried. Elvira looks triumphant, then realizes her triumph means that she's right about her mother becoming a mass of jelly molded only by a nylon suit.

"Tell you what," says the man, checking his watch, "they're just about due to float down. Let's go pick them up and you can see for yourself that your mom is all in one piece."

The man gently pulls the coffee cup from Elvira's hands and sets it down. They walk outside the hangar and stand close together, looking skyward while shielding their eyes from the afternoon sun with uplifted arms. But instead of seeing two white pillows with tiny G.I. Joe-looking figures wisping through the air in the distance, they see only the airplane coming in for a landing.

"What does it mean?" asks Elvira. The man is calm, although his face betrays concern.

"Nothing," he says, and takes Elvira by the arm as they head toward the airplane.

Elvira expects the pilot to exit the plane in a panic, waving his arms in despair because he has lost two jumpers and demanding that a search party be formed immediately. Instead, the plane comes to a stop, the engine rests, and the belly door opens. There stands Elvira's mother, Brubaker gallantly holding her about the waist, and they smile at each other as they step away from the machine of doom.

Elvira's comforter beats her to the question. "What happened?"

"Damnedest luck," answers Brubaker. "We were just about to make our jump and your mother twisted her ankle." Mother smiles reassuringly. "Not a thing to worry about," she says. "I'll be right as rain and ready to go again in no time at all." Brubaker is obviously content that what she says is the gospel and grins back at her as Elvira and her consoler move in to help Brubaker assist the woman to the car.

Once settled, Elvira's mother adjusts her perfect, petite, unbruised, unswollen ankle into a comfortable position on the carpeted floorboard. Brubaker leans into the passenger-side window and admonishes Elvira's mother to see a doctor immediately. He mentions applying ice, elevating the foot, avoiding movement for the next few days.

The young man wishes the women well, then recommends that Elvira look into skydiving lessons, that he would be pleased to help her with the information. She promises him that she will call, and she means it, but decides she will tell him sometime in the future that she would rather become a snake handler than learn to skydive. The women leave the two men standing on the tarmac, both of them waving a safe trip home, and Brubaker calling out that he will telephone Elvira's mother later.

"Should we go see Tía Salina at the hospital?" Elvira asks her mother, as the men they've left behind become miniature in the rearview mirror.

"No, es nada," answers Mother. "A few days with it on the pillow and a little ice, everything will be fine. You should not worry so much, mijita. I am able to take care of myself."

Border Crossing

Every autumn the women of El Nido take up the task of canning the bounty of fruits and vegetables grown during the summer. Mason jars are moved to the fronts of grocery stores and women converge on them as if the stores have set them out for free. Used jars are gathered from cellars and checked for cracks or chips; if they pass inspection, they're washed and boiled and used again. Whether it's cooking the food itself or steaming the jars, huge canning pots are not given a rest for days at a time.

Apricots are washed, cut in half, pitted, and dowsed with sugar for making winter pies. Suffused with seasoning, cucumbers miraculously become pickles. Fresh sweet corn is shaved off the cob and mixed with red pimiento so it will look colorful and tempting on the cellar shelf. Beet greens are pulled from the purple bulb, washed, and refrigerated for salad, while the beet itself is chopped, cooked, and stuffed into jars. The last of the season's carrots, onions, and potatoes are dug from warm earth and tucked inside burlap sacks to lie on cellar shelves until strong female hands snatch them from their repose and sacrifice them to the bodies of their families.

In the Móntez family it was the custom for all the women to do canning together. This day, Yolanda Móntez arrived at the home of her mother-in-law before the other women in her husband's family to make sure no one would say she hadn't earned her share of the canning at the end of the chore. A covey of children followed behind her as she passed through the side gate and into the yard. Her son, Óscar, born while she was a young unmarried girl in Mexico, carried the baby's necessities in a grocery sack. Yolanda's three girls lugged toys. Yolanda always kept Óscar beside her, even if it was only to hang out laundry. That way no one could say anything to him to hurt his feelings. Yolanda settled Óscar and his three half-sisters on the lawn with blocks and dolls and crayons and paper. She strapped the baby, also a girl, to her middle and walked into her mother-in-law's kitchen to begin washing apricots. Yolanda liked physical labor; she was used to it and it kept her mind busy.

Soon, Yolanda's sisters-in-law began to arrive and the kitchen became a din of chatter and gossip and instructions. Yolanda enjoyed the company of the women in her husband's family sometimes, but she knew also what they thought of her. They believed her to be backward and cowering and simple, and they knew that these things were why Jaime had gone to Mexico to find her. And, Yolanda often thought, they were right.

She missed Mexico. Not the poor pay and the Sonora Desert dirt that had to be constantly swept away, of course, but she missed her mother, her brothers and sisters, and the beauty of Guaymas. She also missed herself being there. In Mexico she had not seemed so simple and backward.

Jaime was different there too. He had brought her gifts and gently patted the top of her son's head. He sat in her parents' home talking for hours to her father, eating at the family table, complimenting her mother's tortillas as the lightest he had ever had, then, with mock fear of retribution, made everyone at the table promise not to tell his mother he had said such a thing. Yolanda's friends and family envied that she would be going to the United States, and they cried like children the day Jaime took her away. Yolanda beamed as she waved good-bye, betraying that she too felt her circumstances worthy of the envy. Yoly did not know, as she shed tears of expectant happiness, that the sadnesses and disappointments of life do not end simply because someone crosses a border. Those can be found everywhere; they are as mobile as the mind.

The business of canning fell into a routine as each woman was given tasks according to her liking and ability. One of the sisters-in-law had small hands, so she washed the jars. Another sister washed the produce, while the one standing next to her whittled it to fit inside the jars.

One of Yolanda's labors was to carry her mother-in-law's canned goods to the cellar because the steps were impossible for the old woman's arthritic knees. Yolanda's first trip to the cellar caught the attention of her children and they fell in behind her, laughing and dirt-streaked, wanting to help. After setting down the box of food, she handed each child a jar and told them to hold it very close so it would not slip from tiny hands. Yolanda then opened the cellar door.

The afternoon sun spread across the floor of the cellar and at the bottom of the steps lay a cat staring up at Yolanda. Her children saw it too and wondered at its stillness. "What happened to the kitty, Mamá?" they chorused. Yolanda took a breath and then explained that the cat must have gotten into the cellar a couple of weeks before, when she was collecting the jars to be washed for the canning. She did not tell her children, but she now remembered leaving the door open while she walked back to the house with her arms full of jars, not returning until dark, several hours later. The cat must have been in the cellar when she closed the door.

Yolanda found herself wanting to touch the cat, to pet it. She began thinking of what might have happened while the cat was trapped in the cellar. She imagined that the cat must have thought the cellar seemed like a playground at first. There were lots of places to explore. Shelves of varying heights, almost empty of last year's harvest, must have let it test its leaping. An earthen mound separating the food from a crawl space meant for replacing ancient pipes probably offered cool virgin dirt for digging and disposing, and respite from summer's last swelters. There was enough light from a screened vent to allow sight and ventilation—but no escape. After a while the cat must have realized the playground was really a prison. It must have meowed and scratched at the vent, perhaps even trying to bite through it. It might have given up on escape and reconciled itself to the hope of finding nourishment and water within its cell walls.

But hope was futile. No water dripped from the pipes and no mice made their way through the steel meshing carefully stuffed into cracks. It must have clawed furiously at every surface because its paws were rubbed clean of fur at the toe tips and small droplets of blood were dried at the end of each ragged nail. The paws were the only puffy parts on the animal; the rest of its body looked like a piece of fleshy fruit dried in the sun. The fur lay flat and matted against collapsed bones, the face shrunken back from bulging eyes frozen in frenzied despair.

Óscar watched his mother's shoulders begin to shake and watched her face twist into the same face she once wore when he had cut his foot on a piece of glass and Yolanda rushed him to the doctor for stitches. Then it seemed as if her legs would no longer hold her and Yolanda sat down on the ground and put a hand to her throat to strangle the sound of sorrow. This frightened her children and soon a wail of children's tears floated into the house where the other women were working.

Yolanda's eldest sister-in-law came out the back door to see what was the matter. She walked up to the congregation of mourners and asked them why they were crying, and Óscar pointed to the dead cat. The woman looked inside the cellar at the cat, then looked at Yolanda, who was now trying to comfort the tears of her children, and walked back into the house. Yolanda heard her say, "Es nada. They are crying over nothing but a useless cat." And the women went back to putting things inside of jars.

Heart's Desire

T he wedding reception of Yolanda Montalvo and Jaime Móntez was held at the National Guard Armory mess hall. No one else was desperate enough to reserve the armory for the end of August, so it had been easy to get. The end of September would have been a much better time for holding a reception at the armory since the outside temperature would have been a good twelve degrees cooler, but if they had waited, Yolanda would not have fit into her pale yellow wedding dress.

The women of Jaime's family had unlocked the heavy gates of the compound and decorated them with yellow ribbons and white balloons. Inside the mess hall, the women had done all they could to disguise the ugly green walls by hanging home-painted banners with Jaime and Yolanda's names entwined in hearts and singing birds. The birds looked more like beetles donning feathers but no matter; the sentiment was the same. The sturdy metal tables were covered in yellow crepe paper and set with rosettes twisted out of tissue just like the ones pictured in the June issue of *Woman's Day* magazine.

Tables pushed against the wall supported roasters filled with pinto beans, green chile made with lean pork, and steamed tamales. Jaime's mother and sisters, with flour sacks wrapped around their middles to protect the silk and chiffon of their wedding attire, were in the armory kitchen making tortillas and cutting tomatoes picked from their gardens for fresh salsa. The full flames under the tortilla flats drove the temperature in the mess hall up another eight degrees.

Isaac Chacón and his band, the Latin Express, played for free because he and Jaime had been friends since childhood and had even managed to do time in Santa Fe State Prison together. They'd each served two years and walked out of one of the toughest prisons in the country vowing never to return. After three years of parole and no violations, the state of New Mexico had pronounced them successfully rehabilitated. Jaime and Isaac believed the state of New Mexico had successfully scared the shit out of them and decided that stealing tires wasn't their line of work. Actually, Isaac and his band played a lot of gigs for free because everybody had known everybody since childhood and the band wasn't good enough to get paying jobs, anyway. It wasn't uncommon that the band would begin to play a song, then Isaac would wave his hand in disgust and say, "Coyotes estúpidos, la canción es 'De Colores.' Bueno, start again. This time together."

The first glimpse of Yolanda for the people of El Nido had been at Our Lady of the Virgen de Guadalupe church. She loosely held the arm of Jaime's father while the old man stolidly escorted her down the aisle. She was smiling as she walked, but her head was down, so the smile was given for no one in particular. Her teeth were white but set widely apart, as if she had been allotted only so many and the hand of genetics had placed them where they would do the most good. The arrangement made her smile resemble a friendly jack-o-lantern. Her long black hair had been piled high, each roll looking as if it supported a Budweiser can beneath it, and two Shirley Temple curls hung at either side of her face. One of Jaime's sisters was a beautician and there was no doubt in anyone's mind that she was the one responsible for Yolanda's hair.

Everyone had heard that Jaime had gone to Mexico to find a bride because he wanted a woman who knew who was boss and "how to keep her mouth shut." Somebody had a cousin who had a cousin by marriage who knew a family in Mexico who had a

neighbor who had an unmarried daughter of tolerable appearance
and a male child out of wedlock and who was properly ashamed
so that she would have to accept any offer of legitimacy, and that's
how Jaime found Yolanda. What Jaime had not counted on was that
Yolanda truly fell in love with him and would have married him
without the promise of going to the United States to live the good
life. Yolanda believed that the conversations with her father and the
compliments to her mother were sincere. She believed that when
Jaime patted the top of her son's head, it meant he was a kind man,
forgiving of her past, and accepting of a future that included her son.
What she did not know was that Jaime came to Mexico knowing she
had a son because he believed it meant she would produce more.

At the reception Yolanda held her hand over her mouth when
she laughed, moved her eyes from one new face to the next with
timid curiosity, and consistently turned an abiding smile toward
her husband as she watched everything he did, listened to every
word he spoke. Yoly's new life had begun.

———————— ◆ ————————

Yoly's new home was a shack one mile outside of El Nido, up
Pump Canyon Road. Only the most tenacious scrub brush
survived in the alkaline soil, but Yoly managed to bring color to
the scenery by planting petunias in little fractured pots and setting
them under windows and along both sides of the front door. She
and her small son hauled conglomerate rocks from the nearby
arroyo and made a welcoming walkway leading to the house.

Yoly's nearest neighbor was Salina Gonzales, a nurse who
worked the swing shift at San Juan Hospital. Salina had grown children and a husband who cared little for her comings and goings.

One day, while Yolanda and her son were carrying rocks from
the arroyo, Salina saw them from her house and went over to say
hello, which turned out to be a little more difficult than Salina
thought it was going to be since Yoly knew very little English and

Salina's Spanish was rusty and outdated. Salina's parents were worried that their children would speak English with an accent, so the only time Salina had heard Spanish when she was growing up was when her parents were angry with each other or planning a surprise for the children.

Salina and Yolanda mainly smiled a lot and pointed and made Oscar laugh with the way they'd cock their heads trying to understand each other. They even tried saying words more slowly and loudly to each other as if that would miraculously transform the words into the other's language, then realized how ridiculous the thought had been and joined Oscar in embarrassed but hearty laughter.

The second time Salina visited Yolanda, the women managed to talk for three hours. They had to use their hands to draw pictures in the air, or pick up objects to demonstrate nouns, or body movements to act out verbs, but when the time was spent, they had become friends.

The women made fun of people they knew by mimicking their figures and affectations. Salina played the part of Jaime's mother by first sticking out her rump, then running into Yoly's bathroom and stuffing towels down the back of her jeans and the front of her shirt to resemble the old woman's massive swells of buttocks and breasts. She raised her nose in the air and clucked her tongue while delivering biting commentary about every family residing in San Juan County just like la Señora Móntez until Yoly was holding her stomach and begging her to stop. "Alto, alto," implored Yoly, her jack-o-lantern smile both beautiful and mischievous.

It was Yoly's turn next. She stuffed a washcloth down the front of her jeans, rolled up like a giant penis, puffed out her chest, and barked orders in Spanish. "Tráeme una cerveza . . . Ayúdame con mis botas . . . Haz los tamales." Salina watched the pantomime and at first she laughed. Then she realized that the performance was as accurate of Jaime as her own had been of Señora Móntez and stood quietly.

"Es mi Jaime," Yoly said, afraid Salina wasn't understanding.

"Yes. Sí," said Salina, forcing a smile to her lips, and she laughed very loudly.

A month passed before Yoly saw Salina again because Salina had been working the night shift at the hospital and sleeping during the day. Then one day Salina walked to Yoly's house to tell her that she would be having a barbecue the following weekend, a celebration to burn Zozobra. She was working right now on stuffing the straw into old clothes and making a face for the effigy. Salina said that after everyone had eaten at the barbecue, they would put a torch to "Old Man Gloom" to burn away the evil spirits and weariness that often come with the winter months. Of course the big fiesta to burn Old Man Gloom always took place in Santa Fe every October, but Salina said she could have her own burning of Zozobra if she damned well wanted to. Salina made Yoly promise to make Jaime bring her. Yoly promised, and when the occasion arrived, Salina watched from the window as her neighbors crossed the arroyo.

Much to Yolanda's embarrassment, Jaime strutted and passed out cheap cigars printed with "It's a Boy" on the cellophane at the barbecue. Yoly still had five months of pregnancy to go and no tests had been done to support Jaime's boast; it all rested only on his belief that Yoly was a producer of males. In confidence, Yoly too believed that the next child would be a boy because she felt the same way she had when she was pregnant with Oscar, and she'd heard that pregnancies with boy babies were different than pregnancies with girl babies. She was content that this one felt like a boy.

Baby showers weren't unheard of in San Juan County, but poor women seemed to have a hard time putting one together. Women worked different shifts, got paid at different times, had husbands who objected, small children who demanded all and more, lives that took too much time from them to have any energy left over. It was more common that, in the months following a birth, women just sort of showed up with little gifts or a box of diapers and stayed for coffee; and they often stayed to help scrub the kitchen floor or hang laundry because helping with chores was considered a present too.

Salina came to Yolanda's house with two tiny pink T-shirts rolled inside the comic section of the newspaper and tied with used Christmas ribbon. Yoly said she loved the wrapping paper—it would help her learn more English humor. Salina told her not to count on the funny papers for a real understanding. In the months since Yoly and Salina had become friends, Yoly had learned English quickly, although she still used mostly the present tense and the women often misunderstood whether something had already happened or was going to happen.

After Yoly unwrapped the T-shirts and smiled at the tiny size, she made coffee and white-bread toast. Salina asked her how she was feeling and Yoly answered that she felt fine, just a little tired. Then she began to cry.

"Mi Jaime está enojado conmigo," said Yoly, holding her baby close to her.

"Why is Jaime mad at you?" asked Salina, putting down her coffee mug and stretching a hand across the table in case Yoly wanted to take it.

"Porque the baby es una girl," whispered Yoly.

Salina took back the hand she had extended and waved it in the air as if shooing a fly. "Ah, they're all like that at first," said Salina. "He'll get over it in time."

Yoly looked unconvinced. "Besides," said Salina feebly, "this won't be your last child." Then, looking angry, she added, "And it's his fault if it's girl anyway. It's simple biology."

"Biología," said Yoly, her face wrinkled into a network of confusion.

"Biology," repeated Salina, "X's and Y's, Yoly. The man's sperm decides the sex of the child."

"The esperma makes the baby girl or boy?" wondered Yoly. Yes, Salina had answered, and at the same moment she said it, she felt an uneasiness.

A few days later Salina went to Yolanda's house to share coffee and found that Yoly did not feel like talking. Yoly stood at the door without opening it wider than one side of her body and told Salina they would have coffee some other time. Salina walked away wondering if she and Yoly were still friends and wondering what she had done that would make Yolanda guard the opening of her house so closely.

A week later, Yolanda carried her baby while Óscar skipped beside her and they walked to Salina's house. It had been enough time that the bruises on Yolanda's arms had faded to a greenish yellow and she wore a long-sleeved blouse. After the two women had settled down with warm mugs and Salina had given Oscar a comic book, Yoly told Salina she wasn't allowed to talk about biology anymore. She had told Jaime about the X's and Y's, hoping he would forgive her for having a girl but that was not how Jaime took the information at all. Yoly didn't tell Salina about this; she only said no more biology and that it would be better if Salina didn't come over for a while. Yoly also told her that she was pregnant again.

After Yoly had her second daughter, Salina was allowed to come back over, but she usually waited until Jaime's car drove away before she went. After Yolanda's third daughter was born, Salina was again banished from the house because Yolanda had stayed too long at Salina's one day and didn't have Jaime's dinner ready when he pulled up from work. Jaime had crossed the arroyo and banged on Salina's door, hollering for Yolanda and shouting at her all the way home that a man had a right to expect certain things. Salina had tried to defend Yoly, but this was one of those times when a person wanted to be mad, so there's really not much another person can say when someone is determined to stay that way. Salina told Jaime as much too. First she tried telling him not to be angry because it was really all her fault that Yoly had stayed too long. But Jaime just went on shouting at Yoly until Salina hollered after him as he was walking away, "Ah, pendejo cabrón, you would whine if your ice cream was cold," which pretty much got Salina banned from Yolanda's house for life.

When the fourth girl was born, Salina watched Jaime's car pull away from the house, then walked over to Yoly's carrying a package. Yolanda gave Salina coffee, then sat down to unwrap the package and looked very pleased to find a lipstick pencil, a tube of eyeliner, and a small case of beige eyeshadow.

"I thought it was about time you were the one getting a gift instead of the baby," said Salina, smiling. Yolanda smiled back and asked Salina to show her how to use the eye shadow.

"Does Jaime like you with makeup?" asked Salina. Yoly couldn't answer right away because Salina had her stretching her lips wide while she applied red lip liner to her mouth. Salina pulled away, poising the lip pencil in the air and assessing her work.

"Sí, he like it," said Yoly. "Pero I no have so much time for the makeup."

Salina looked around Yoly's house—clean but cluttered with children's toys, fresh laundry yet unfolded and the children themselves, and wondered how she kept any order at all in the two-bedroom house holding a family of seven.

She picked up a tube of lipstick and began filling in the lines drawn on Yoly's lips as Yoly obediently stretched her mouth taut again.

"Do you ever think about not having any more babies?" asked Salina as nonchalantly as she could. She knew it was a question that would embarrass her friend, but sweet Yolanda answered anyway.

"Oh sí, I think about it a lot. I wish about it a lot."

"Hold still," said Salina, fastening a pair of fashion earrings through Yoly's pierced ears.

"Is it the money, Yoly? They have certain programs at the hospital where you can get free birth control, or even one of those tubal things. Comprendes the tubal thing?"

"Sí, comprendo, pero I no can do it, amiga." Yoly picked up a hand mirror and looked at herself, pleased but unsmiling.

"Of course you can. I could loan you the money. I'll *give* you the money. We'll make up some kind of lie for Jaime. Men were meant to be lied to; they bring it on themselves. They . . ."

Yoly had begun shaking her head before Salina ever finished her sentence. "You no understand, amiga, Jaime will no let me."

"Jesus, Yoly, this is America, the twentieth century. Does he expect you to keep having babies until you run out of eggs!"

"No, amiga, just until I have a boy."

Following the birth of her fourth female child, Yoly went for three years without getting pregnant; but after Jaime started asking questions, she threw away the pills Salina had brought to her and it wasn't long before she felt the familiar changes in her body. By that time she was thirty-four years old and even the doctors in Farmington had begun demanding certain tests for every pregnant woman over the age of thirty. Yoly's tests revealed that her next child was healthy and that it was to be a boy. Jaime bought a fresh stock of cheap cigars.

A celebration was planned to take place at the little Móntez house. Jaime was so filled with good humor at the thought of his forthcoming son that he lifted Salina's banishment and allowed her to attend. Again the Móntez women descended into Yolanda's life, decorating the little house with blue streamers, setting up picnic tables bulging with platters of food. A young goat, gutted and stuffed with garlic, had been buried in the ground, covered with wet leaves and hot coals, and left there to roast for thirty hours. When it was exhumed, the meat was so tender, it fell from the bones with barely the prick of a fork. Isaac Chacón and the band played well into the night, sounding better and better with each pass of the tequila. The revelers stayed late and drove away fat from the food, half drunk from the tequila, and filthy from dancing in the barren dirt outside Yoly's house. Jaime had fallen asleep beside the bonfire, clutching a bottle, cigars spilling out of his shirt pocket.

Salina and Yoly sat in folding chairs in front of the dying fire, holding sleeping children and laughing once again at the jokes told at the party. Then they sat quietly watching the sparks fly into the air like lightning bugs.

"The sleep of children is sweet," said Yoly, looking down at her youngest child.

"And so are the dreams of a fool," answered Salina. It was a New Mexico expression. If someone called you a fool, the retort was always "Then you must envy me, for a fool's dreams are untroubled."

Yoly and Salina said nothing more, but both women looked over at Jaime.

Some months later Yoly woke Jaime, telling him that the child would soon be born and they'd better start the forty-minute trip to the hospital. Jaime roused himself, complaining that she had never given birth during daylight. While Jaime attempted to stuff his foot into the wrong shoe, Yoly found a flashlight, slipped on a coat, and held her stomach while she walked to over to wake the teenage daughter of a neighbor. The girl had promised to watch the children when the time came, and she and Yoly walked back to the house whispering agreement on what the children should eat for breakfast. Salina was working the night shift at the hospital and Yoly hoped she would be able to say hello to her when she got there.

It was March and the El Nido Highway was slick with frozen dew, so Jaime drove slowly. Yoly sat next to him, resting her head on his shoulder; she squeezed his leg and whispered, "You will soon have your boy, mi corazón." A moment later a small sound like the intake of breath punctuated by a hiccup escaped her throat and Yoly lay still for the rest of the trip. Her hand remained on Jaime's leg, but was more relaxed. Jaime reached across her belly and pinched a handful of her outer thigh and returned his hand to the steering wheel. Yoly didn't seem to notice and they drove on in silence.

The lights over the emergency entrance illuminated an empty driveway and Jaime thought that perhaps Yoly's timing wasn't so bad after all. He pulled the car up to the entrance, shaking his shoulder up and down a few times to make Yolanda wake up. "Mira, Yolanda, estamos en el hospital." Yolanda's head only bobbed up and down with the shoulder, and Jaime wondered out loud how it was that a woman could sleep through labor "after all that complaining about how much it hurt."

Two nurses came toward the sliding glass doors to see what kind of trouble had pulled into the driveway and Jaime pushed Yolanda's head away, leaving it to rest on the back of the seat while he opened the car door. He smiled at the nurses over the top of the car and recognized Salina as one of the women on duty. "Hola, Salina. Oye, she's in labor, pero she's asleep."

Both nurses looked at Jaime with wide eyes, looked at each other, and lunged for the passenger side door.

"Get a gurney," screamed Salina, who'd made it inside the car first. She grabbed Yoly's wrist, then put two fingers to her throat.

"How long?" shouted Salina at Jaime, who was bent over, looking back into the car.

"How long?" repeated Jaime stupidly.

"How long has she been like this?"

"You mean asleep?" said Jaime as he watched Salina punch Yoly in the chest.

"How long, you idiot!" spat Salina and punched Yolanda again. Yoly's body simply recoiled against the car seat. Her head bounced off the upholstery and came to rest at a twisted angle, making her neck look broken. The red lights spelling out "Emergency Entrance" neutralized the blue tint of her skin.

"Thirty minutes," said Jaime through clenched teeth.

The gurney arrived with the other nurse and a doctor, and they pulled Yoly out of the car. Salina began blowing air into Yoly's mouth while the doctor pushed on her chest, all of them steering the gurney through the doors and leaving Jaime standing alone in the glow of the emergency lights.

"Is the baby going to be all right?" Jaime hollered. "Is *she* going to be all right?" he shouted to the backs of the people helping his wife, now almost too far away to hear. The words echoed off the glass doors and floated into the night like balloons set free by a careless child.

It was the policy of the *Farmington Daily Times* to announce births and deaths at no charge to the families. A family member need only call to have a funeral announced. Births were even simpler. The information was gleaned over the phone from the hospital receptionist early every morning and printed the following day. And so it was written, and appeared in the newspaper on the same day, that Yolanda María Esteban Montalvo Móntez had died, and that a healthy son had been born to her.

The Redeemer

A lice drove into El Nido not knowing where she was and wondering what kind of simple-minded people would live in such a place. She'd driven the whole length of the town in a little more than a mile, and within that mile there were fewer than twenty homes on the main highway and perhaps five buildings where signs announced businesses. Well, really only four because the gas station was attached to the ammunition and hunting supply store, and the post office was inside that. Down the road was a bar, and sitting a little more than fifteen hundred feet from the bar was a church. But Alice wouldn't be going into the church and the bar didn't open until three o'clock on week-days. Right now she needed cigarettes and directions to the next town. It was unclear to her that to get to the next town she need only keep moving in the same direction on Highway 46 she'd been going; she knew only that there hadn't been a sign since she'd seen three men changing a flat tire near a post marking the boarded-up hamlet of Govenador.

Alice sat in her car checking her lipstick and rubbing a smudge of mascara from beneath her eye before walking into Lobato's Grocery. She hesitated when she saw a scrawny man with dirty clothes and an inadequate, pubic-looking beard enter the store, but then she shrugged and opened the car door. The man didn't look healthy enough to be a danger, so she followed him into the store, unavoidably whiffing the stench of stale alcohol and an unwashed body.

Inside the store a short, middle-aged woman with glasses and black hair belying her real color stood behind the counter. Children scampered from a kitchen where a television blared and back again into the grocery. An old woman leaned against a cane as she spoke quietly with the woman behind the counter. Mrs. Lobato and Hortencia Alcón often spent part of an afternoon discussing the town's goings-on.

In one corner of the store stood a couple huddled shoulder to shoulder with hands entwined, discussing the limited selection of products set before them on a crowded shelf. The couple was young, the man dressed in cowboy boots and jeans, a black felt Resistol hat set firmly on his head. The woman had beautiful red hair and white skin without the freckles that usually accompany such hair, long legs, and wore no more makeup than a touch of lipstick.

Alice heard the dirty man boom out a hello to the couple and watched him disappear behind a rack of packaged snacks. "Hey, Auggie, hey, Leeree. How you doin'?" The man bounced on the balls of his feet back toward the couple.

"Hey, Bubbles," said the man. The woman smiled.

"Did ya heaw, Byoomfeld Betty got otta da hosbidal. Ain't dat sum kind a ga damned . . ." The scrawny man cut a look at the old women at the counter and tipped a filthy baseball cap in their direction. "Ain't dat a miweecal?"

The alcohol-hoarse voice with the funny speech impediment thundered in the small store. Mrs. Lobato and Hortencia Alcón stopped their conversation, the children stood sewn to a spot between the grocery and the back room, and Alice wondered if perhaps she should drive on and stop at a stranger's house to get directions.

"Yeah, she gonna make ot, man. And dey caught da guys dat did ot."

Agustín winced with embarrassment at the volume of Bubbles's voice and the content of his language and tried to serve as an example by keeping his voice low.

"That's great news, Bubbles. Glad to hear it."

It did no good. Bubbles bellowed his way into the next sentence as if everyone in the store had been stricken with a hearing loss.

"Yep, two touwsand stitches, inside and out," said Bubbles, shaking his head. "Sum-gun, she's a tough bwoad, ain't she?"

As much as it pained him, the cowboy moved to close the gap between Bubbles and himself in yet another futile attempt to get Bubbles to quiet his voice. The couple breathed through their mouths, trying to keep as much of Bubbles's smell out of their nostrils as possible. Mrs. Lobato looked at the woman who'd entered her store in Bubbles's wake and intended to wave her to the cash register so the woman might leave as quickly as possible. But Alice stood transfixed on the man, listening to the story of some tragic woman whose body now held two thousand stitches because of some psychotic men, and thank God they'd been caught.

Bubbles went on to describe how the doctors had managed to stuff Betty's bowels back inside her skin "almos' in da same pwace dey was befowe." While everyone watched him fill a plastic bag full of red potatoes, Bubbles elaborated on Betty's bowels, saying the doctors had to cut off five feet of intestine to get everything closed up inside Betty's belly. He then turned toward the bread rack and reached for a fifty-cent loaf of day-old white bread. As he did, the overfilled bag of potatoes burst at the seams and sent spuds rolling in six directions at once. The couple bent down to retrieve the vegetables rolling closest to them while Bubbles chased the strays and hollered over his shoulder that the hunting knife had missed the pancreas.

"Funny how dey can't get evweething back jus' da way it was afta' it's been cut open," said Bubbles as he ducked under a display of Old Milwaukee beer to retrieve a potato.

"Kinda wike Chwistmas wights afta ya get 'em oudda da box. Ya evva nodiced dat? Ya nevva can get 'em back in da box again, all kuwled up nice and neat wike when ya bwought 'em. Ya use-ly end up thwoein' dem in a bag or a bigga box or sum-fing."

Alice had difficulty imagining the little man *buying* Christmas lights, much less stringing them around a tree without pulling the whole thing down upon himself.

Mrs. Lobato called out to her grandchildren to go back into the room where the television blared and close the door, then chided Bubbles under her breath in Spanish for having no shame in front of children. Bubbles simply popped his head up from behind a stack of cantaloupe and continued his tale regarding the miraculous recovery of Betty.

"She got ta keep almos' all her stwomach, doe."

Bubbles had potatoes stuffed under his armpits while he juggled and dropped several more. Agustín tore off two plastic bags from the roll and helped Bubbles deposit the potatoes inside. Lily, the cowboy's wife, was too mesmerized by the whole scene to be of much help and stood holding one potato until her husband slipped it out of her hand and placed it in the bag along with the others.

Bubbles took the potatoes and headed toward the bologna. "I gotta go, you guys," said Bubbles as if were the fault of the congregation that he had stayed talking too long. He plopped the groceries on the counter and Mrs. Lobato rang them up quickly. Hortencia Alcón moved back a few steps and covered her nose with an embroidered handkerchief.

The little man whisked himself through the door, leaving behind a store full of people feeling as if they'd run a marathon. Mrs. Lobato and Mrs. Alcón went back to whispering the gossip of El Nido while Alice moved toward the counter to ask for cigarettes and directions. As she moved, she heard the red-haired woman ask her husband, "Who is Betty and what in God's name happened to her?" The man took his wife's hand and said that they should hurry with the baking powder or his mother would be unable to make the tortillas in time for dinner.

Alice reached the counter before the couple and asked for a pack of Virginia Slims. "Also, can you please tell me if I'm on the right road for Durango?"

"Well," answered Mrs. Lobato, "you are on the right road to get to the right road."

Alice crooked her head and Hortencia Alcón jumped in. "You keep going straight until you get to Bloomfield. Then you make a right turn—north. That road will take you into Durango."

"Bloomfield. Where do I turn? Which road in Bloomfield?"

"When you come to the stoplight. It's the only one. Just make a right at the stoplight," said the old woman, waving her right arm in the air and pointing west.

"Thank you," said Alice, and she left the store and entered the only phone booth in El Nido. After putting in the change and asking for the room number she wanted, she counted the rings for a whole minute, then replaced the receiver.

Putting the car into drive, she reeled the scene she'd witnessed in the store through her mind again and thought of how ridiculous it was for people to live in such a stupid little town where dirty little men reeking of alcohol and stale sweat could just go about. She looked first at one side of the road, then the other, thinking of how desolate the place seemed, and within the trance of her judgment she missed the sight of antelope grazing at the top of a hill. She missed El Huerfano standing in the distance guarding the base of the great Rocky Mountain plateau, and she missed the cottonwoods along the mighty San Juan River where ducks and geese and salmon made common appearances. She missed a bald eagle swooping from a tree above the San Juan and catching a fish in his talons, then majestically laboring his great wings back into the air.

These things she missed because small towns and the ordinary movements of life sustaining itself did not interest her. She was in a hurry to see her lover, to get away from the husband who took such good care of her but who bored her because he was faithful and always on time and always a little afraid she might leave him—just as she was doing now.

A gustín and Lily climbed into the pickup truck and headed toward the Pump Canyon turnoff. The road meandered before them like an old friend full of anecdotes, and the couple settled into a comfortable silence for several miles. They saw women sweeping doorways, noted dogs sleeping in the sun, and became momentarily hypnotized by the furrows of newly ploughed fields, as if the rows themselves were the ones speeding past. They saw Yolanda Móntez, swollen with child yet again, picking chile pods from the ristra trussed to the beam of her porch. They observed the Carters' perennially dirty children playing in the grass-barren yard. Rusted-out cars had been turned into forts where the children devised plots for catapulting filth at one another; the mounds of trash were hills used for hiding behind and mounting attacks. Drooping Christmas lights hung from the eaves although it was the end of March.

"She gave me her lunch," said Agustín, breaking the silence.

Lily pulled her mind away from planning a garden, wondering if she'd heard her husband correctly. "What, honey? When did you miss lunch?"

"Betty. Betty shared her lunch with me . . . in the second grade . . . I'd forgotten mine."

Lily watched her husband's eyes blink rapidly behind his sunglasses.

"I didn't really know her, but she saw me not eating and gave me half her lunch."

The couple rounded the last bend before their turnoff and came to a stop behind a short row of other pickup trucks waiting for a flock of sheep to cross the road. An ancient Navajo sheep-herder with a face as chiseled and dry as the mesas in the distance pulled himself along with a cane cut from a cottonwood tree.

"She came to school with welts on her legs a lot. . . . Once, with a black eye."

Agustín adjusted his sunglasses and swallowed as if he was forcing a piece of half-chewed meat down his throat.

"We were just little kids, you know. You say whatever comes into your mind when you're a kid," said Agustín. "So I asked what happened. She said . . . ah . . . she said . . ."

Lily stared at her husband, waiting for the words. "What did she say, Agustín?"

"Even then, young like that . . . little kids . . . the thing she said kinda stunned me . . . you know?"

The couple drove past the Rodríguez house and waved at Salina as she struggled with grocery bags.

"Honey, what did she say?"

"'I'm a bad girl.'"

The farm came into sight and the pickup rumbled across the cattle guard and rolled down the dirt drive as chickens ran for their lives ahead of it.

The pickup came to a stop and Agustín shut it down with a strong shift of the gear handle and a flip of the key ring.

"You've never talked about her before," said Lily.

Agustín took the bag containing the baking powder and opened the door to get out. He looked back at his wife and said only, "She's been talked about enough," then he never spoke of Betty again.

It was true. Bloomfield Betty had been talked about enough. She grew up to be exactly what she called herself—a bad girl. And whether the people knew it or not, they loved her for it. They loved her because no matter what, no one was as bad as Betty. She provided jokes for the men, proof of the devil for Christian women, and redemption for women who had their own reputations to live down. Bloomfield High School was where all the kids from El Nido and Largo Canyon and Arboleta were bused once they had finished grade school and it was then that Betty got her name from the porno films released in the seventies like *Holly Does Hollywood* and *Debbie Does Dallas*.

Betty had done Bloomfield.

Parties planned specially for Betty took place in the shallow hills between Bloomfield and El Nido. There she danced in the moonlight without her clothes, taking swallows of beer and liquor from bottles held by faceless boys who waited for Betty's dance to end—then waited their turn. By the time Betty was eighteen, she had two children born of anonymous sperm, and she decided that the boys of Bloomfield would have to pursue their carnal education elsewhere.

It seems Betty took naturally to mothering. She got her General Education Diploma, got a job at Farmer's Market stocking shelves when the store was closed, and went home every morning after work. She played with her children when she wasn't working and told her father that if he ever hit them she'd kill him in his sleep.

But the snickers and muffled rustle of words never seemed to stop. People refused to forget the past. At twenty years old, Betty left a note addressed to her parents next to her sleeping children and ran away with a carnival barker who resembled her father—except that he had tattoos on his neck and the knuckles of his hands.

Eight months later Betty hitchhiked back to Bloomfield wearing two pairs of athletic socks to keep a set of men's cowboy boots from rubbing blisters on her heels, and supporting a broken arm set in a fetid cast. When she got back she stole from the same shopkeepers who had given her candy when she was a child. She stole from her parents and wrecked their car. She was seen riding in fast-moving cars with men no one knew, men who later split her open and left her lying in a bed of leaves holding her entrails to keep them from falling out and mixing with the dirt.

But that wasn't the worst that Betty did. The worst thing she did was get drunk and go to the houses of the boys she used to know. Boys turned men who were married now, held jobs, had children. Betty stood in their driveways screaming obscenities, screaming crazy things nobody understood about how they'd been forgiven but she hadn't. She'd stood in the driveway screaming those things, a bottle in one hand and chunks of her own hair in the other, until Sheriff Max arrived and loaded her inside his car.

There she slumped against the side window and moaned. "Moaned like a soul trapped in a haunted house," Sheriff Max later told his wife.

No one was as bad as Betty.

A lice drove her Cadillac along the El Nido highway thinking of her home in Alamogordo, where surely her husband had pulled his car into the double garage by now and noticed her stall standing empty. He wouldn't think to start calling their friends or the police or the hospitals for a couple of hours more since he was used to his wife not being there to greet him or leaving a note to say when she'd be back. For a long time now he had let her go without question or reprimand, hoping it was the thing that would keep her. He would not think to look through her closet and count the missing boxes of leather shoes or notice that the beaver coat she usually wore only for special occasions was gone.

Alice's husband would simply stand at the stove warming himself a can of soup while wondering if his wife had had her dinner, then call the dog over to lie next to him on the couch while he balanced his soup bowl with one hand and dipped his spoon with the other.

Alice thought of her lover and hoped he would wait to have dinner with her. When she had called her lover the night before and told him she just couldn't stand it anymore and asked him if he'd meant all those things about the two of them running away and being together, he'd answered that sure he meant it, but she had to remember that he was a traveling man. Why, just look at where he was now, up in Durango, Colorado, and then in a few days on to Salt Lake City, and after that he'd be in west Texas. Couldn't she wait until he got back to New Mexico in another month or so and they could talk about it then? But Alice said that if he meant all those things, then he'd take her with him and people in love just get things figured out. Finally, the lover acquiesced and said now that she put it that way, maybe it was time to talk, and he gave her directions to Durango going through Chama. He'd hung up without saying he loved her or that he couldn't wait to see her. Alice packed her clothes believing that once they were together he would realize that she was right about it being time they were together.

Alice started her trip without checking a map, so she never wondered why the man had said to go through Chama. She'd been too excited to question his directions until it was too late to go through Albuquerque. Then, retrieving a map from the glove box, she realized that he'd sent her a good 150 miles out of her way.

She had stopped in Chama to call and let him know where she was, but after asking for the room number, there was no answer. North of Albuquerque it was much colder than Alamogordo. She hoped for a room with a fireplace and that the lover would have the room cozy for her when she got there. She then realized by the name that the motel was not the sort of place that was going to have fireplaces in the rooms. No matter, they could always move to another motel once she got there. She didn't worry that he wasn't in the room; he was probably just out having a bite to eat or perhaps working extra time on the project. She would call him again from the next town.

She turned the heater on full blast in the Cadillac, then rolled down the window to float a gloved hand through the late-afternoon chill. She was humming to a song on the radio when she saw a woman walking along the curving two-lane highway. Normally, Alice would never consider picking up a person walking alongside the road, but this woman caught her attention because of the way she was dressed. She looked cold. Her coat didn't look warm enough for the spring freeze that was setting in. Her ample bottom romped beneath worn-thin turquoise pants discernibly patched along the center seam. A beaded evening bag hung over her shoulder by one threadbare strap. Watching her sandals flap against her heels made Alice's feet, snuggled inside suede boots with sheepskin lining, suddenly turn cold. She imagined that the woman's heels must be numb, and each slap of the sandal must have felt like a sting.

The woman's face was tinged blue when she crawled into the Cadillac.

"It's too cold to be walking," said Alice as the woman struggled with the heavy door.

"That's for sure," said the woman, showing straight yellow teeth. Her hair hung past her shoulders in oily, thin lines the color of the clay pebbles people pour into litter boxes.

"I'm going to Bloomfield, then to Durango," said Alice.

"That's cool. Bloomfield's cool. Mind if I smoke?"

Alice couldn't really say no since the ashtray was open and several butts lay stubbed inside of it. Alice said she didn't mind, and lit one up along with the woman, although she hadn't thought about smoking until the woman brought it up.

"You live around here?" asked Alice, pulling the ashtray out as far as it would go and praying that the woman had good aim.

"Sometimes," answered the woman.

The woman did not have good aim. She flipped the butt of her cigarette upward with her thumb instead of tapping it with her index finger, which made the ashes do a hop in the air and bounce off the edge of the tray. She settled her round body fully against the back of the leather seat. Everything about her was round. Her head reminded Alice of a ball; her eyes were two clear blue marbles. Even her hands looked as if they were most comfortable clenched into round fists, holding onto something. The woman pulled at the shirt stretched taut across her belly, then rested her hand over her stomach as if comforting a twinge of indigestion.

"Nice car," remarked the woman, swiveling her head to survey the backseat. "You married to someone rich?"

"No," said Alice, "I'm a . . . not married anymore."

The oily-haired woman laughed a sort of seal bark with smoker's lungs. "That's the way to do it. Divorce 'em and keep their stuff. They deserve it."

"Oh, no, he's a very nice man," blurted Alice.

The women rode along for a full two miles in silence, both of them smoking, Alice watching the woman's cigarette ashes out of the corner of her eye.

"You got kids?" asked the round woman. It's the sort of question women ask each other when there is no other common ground.

"No. My husband always wanted them but I've—we've kept putting it off."

"I thought you weren't married."

"I'm not. I mean, well, I'm in the process of getting a divorce."

"Oh," said the woman flatly. "I guess that's hard. I broke up with a guy a few months ago. He drank a lot. . . . And he always got mean when he drank."

Alice nodded, keeping her eyes on the road, uncomfortable with how much the woman was telling her. Alice's husband seldom drank. When he did it was never more than two beers and he always did something lighthearted like twirl Alice around the room or tell silly jokes.

"Do you have children?" asked Alice, wanting to get back to something less personal.

"Yeah, a girl and a boy." Again the woman's voice was flat and she stared out the side window, watching houses float by.

"Do you have pictures of them?" Alice smiled at the woman.

"You wanna see my kids?" The woman opened the battered bag and quickly produced two Olan Mills wallet-sized photographs. She studied the pictures for a second or two before passing them to Alice.

"There's Shane, and that's Starla. I named her Starla because she's gonna be a movie star some day. I just know it."

The boy smiled at Alice, unaware that a few hairs on the back of his head were sticking up, and the girl grinned with a mouthful of missing teeth. Both had their mother's round face and clay-colored hair. Alice pronounced the children adorable and handed back the pictures.

"Where can I drop you off?" asked Alice. The woman said that at the corner when they reached the stoplight would be good enough.

"Where are you going from there?" asked Alice.

"Albuquerque," said the woman.

"Oh, is that where your children are?" asked Alice.

"No, they're here. I mean in El Nido. . . . I just . . . I'm just going for a while. . . . I mean, I'm coming back. . . . Why are you going to Durango?"

"Oh. Well, I just want to get away for a while. I've heard Durango is beautiful."

"Yeah, it is." The woman lit another cigarette. "So where's your husband . . . or ex-husband or whatever?"

"Alamogordo," answered Alice. "We moved there about a year ago for my husband's job. I haven't made any friends, and there's not much to . . ."

"You came through Chama from Alamogordo?"

"How'd you know that?" Alice couldn't keep the surprise out of her voice.

"Only two ways to go to Durango from Alamogordo. But people don't usually take the way you came unless they got family somewhere along the way. Or they're lost." The woman barked the smoker's laugh again.

Alice pulled the car to a stop at the traffic light. While the women waited for the light to change, they looked over at a man hanging a banner announcing the opening of a "Kiddy Karnival" the following week. "Fun for the whole family," it said.

"Will you be back in time to take your kids?" asked Alice brightly. "I bet they'd like that."

The woman stared out the window at the banner. "Maybe. Yeah, I guess they would like it," answered the woman.

"I remember my mother taking me to a carnival when I was a child," said Alice. "Just for that one day she said I could do anything I wanted. She said I could go on all the rides I wanted, as many times as I wanted. And she let me eat ice cream and candy and anything I wanted for the whole day."

Alice smiled at herself in the mirror, then turned the smile on the woman sitting in the passenger seat of her car. "Funny how you remember something like that for the rest of your life, isn't it?"

The woman looked at Alice's face as if there was something written on it, some message she was tediously trying to decipher, then turned and looked out the side window again at the man hanging the banner.

The light changed to green and Alice turned the corner and pulled off the road. The woman tugged at the door handle and shoved open the door.

"Well, hey, thanks for the ride."

"Sure," said Alice, then leaning as far across the front seat as she could without taking her foot off the brake, she called after the woman. "Are you sure you're going to be all right? It's almost dark and it's getting awfully cold. Are you sure you can get a ride?"

"Don't worry," said the woman, shouldering the evening bag, "I'm lucky."

Alice watched the woman cross the street and hold up her thumb. Just ahead stood a phone booth so Alice turned off the car and dug for change. She waved at the woman as she walked to the booth, and the woman waved back. Alice dialed the number in Durango, putting in the correct amount of change, and again asked for the room number. The phone rang and rang until Alice became convinced that she had asked for the wrong room, so she hung up and tried the number again.

Again a man answered the phone, identifying the motel. "I think I've been asking for the wrong room," said Alice. "Would you please connect me with Mr. Dickson's room." The man on the other end told her to hold on, then came back on the line and told Alice that there was no Mr. Dickson staying there.

"But he must be. He's waiting for me."

"Says here he checked out last night."

Alice blinked at the phone as if the object was no longer familiar to her, as if she'd never seen one before. It took a minute, but finally she shuffled to her car and sat behind the steering wheel watching the woman she'd given a ride to walk back across the street. The woman put out her thumb again, this time pointed back in the direction of El Nido.

Again Alice dug in her purse for change, then walked back to the phone booth. She heard her husband's voice and hesitated. "Howard?"

"Alice, honey. I've been so worried. Are you all right?"

"I'm fine, Howard. I just . . . I went for a drive and I . . ."

"Where have you been? Where are you?"

"I . . . um . . . I got lost. . . . I . . ."

"Do you need me to come and get you? Can you find your way back?"

Alice smiled into the phone. "Yes, Howard honey, I know the way back now. And I'll see you in a few hours." Just as she knew he would, Howard asked his wife if she had eaten something. She told him not to worry and the couple said good-bye.

"Oh, and Howard," Alice called into the phone, hoping his hand hadn't cradled the phone and he could still hear her.

"Yes, baby."

"Howard, can we build a fire in the fireplace when I get home?"

"A little warm for a fire, baby," said Howard with a laugh. "But if we have to we'll just open up all the doors and windows."

"Yes, Howard, let's do that."

Alice got back into her car and pointed it south toward Albuquerque. Then, in front of Farmer's Market she turned the car around and turned east on the road headed toward El Nido. The headlights of the Cadillac picked up the silhouette of a woman standing in the dark, shivering, and Alice pulled over. The woman opened the door to the car.

"Thought you were going to Durango," said the woman.

"Thought you were going to Albuquerque," smiled Alice.

"I guess I changed my mind. I can go another time. . . . But if you're going back to Alamogordo you're going way outta your way again."

"That's OK," said Alice.

The woman's eyebrows registered a quick squint.

"I want to give you a ride home."

The woman once again settled herself into Alice's car. She looked inside the beaded purse and brought out a cigarette and some matches.

"My name's Betty," said the woman.

"I know," said Alice. "I met a friend of yours today."

Blue Ruby

In her husband's bureau drawer under some old work shirts, George's wife found a pair of men's bikini underwear with the satin effigy of an elephant's nose hanging from the front. She knew damned well she hadn't bought them and she knew double well that nobody buys something like that who hasn't already seen the elephant's nose underneath the underwear. George's wife set herself on a mission to find more proof that another woman was sharing her life. George, unpracticed at the art of deception until meeting Ruby, provided all she needed.

There were the three bobby pins with several long black strands found alongside the car mat in her husband's El Camino. There was a pack of matches from a bar and grill just over the Colorado state line. There had been the faint waft of an unfamiliar perfume as the wife fanned open the passenger door one morning. Of course, the perfume wasn't physical evidence like the matchbook and bobby pins, but wives count unfamiliar scents as ironclad infidelity evidence, the same as panties rolled up in a bedsheet on wash day.

The wife told George that if he had any ideas about leaving her for some "elephant-nose-underwear-buying tramp," he'd better think again. She reminded him that New Mexico is a community property state and she was going to walk away with her rightful half of his electrical business and get the other half through alimony and child support. Had it slipped his mind they had children together? Did it mean nothing to him that she had forfeited the best years of her life and the firmest flesh of her youth to their marriage? It was beyond her comprehension how she could have married a man who had so little regard for sacrifice.

She told him that just in case he had lost what little sense he'd been born with, well then, he was welcome to his floozy—'cause that was about all he'd have left when she got through with him.

Although the next day wasn't a Wednesday afternoon or a Sunday morning, George called Ruby to say he was coming by to discuss something important. Ruby called a girlfriend to cover her shift at the Pioneer Café, checked her fridge for George's favorite beer, perfumed the sheets, and lay on the couch in her white cotton lace nightie. Every once in a while, George surprised Ruby, and the rendezvous usually meant good news: another contract for his electrical business, a weekend vacation, a new pair of dangly earrings.

George was later getting to Ruby's trailer than he said he'd be. He'd taken the long way, through Aztec, stopping at the Hi-Way Lounge, where he gulped a double bourbon mixed with Coke and took another double in a to-go cup. When he finally arrived, he did not bounce into the room calling, "Where is my Ruby, my gem?" He walked through the front door and stayed standing close to it. For the first few seconds he even left his hand on the knob, twisting it back and forth as if maybe it might suddenly seize up and trap him inside Ruby's trailer house.

He started talking about things Ruby didn't understand, all having to do with math. There were the four children. The multiple problems they'd be bringing on themselves. Something about lousy odds. Half of nothing is still nothing. And what would all the years add up to if he didn't have anything to show for them?

About the closest Ruby had ever come to mastering math was counting her tips at the Pioneer Café and making sure the top figure was bigger than the one just beneath it when she wrote a check. She sat on the couch watching George's mouth move, not really worrying about it because he sometimes got like this, and Ruby thought he was having one of his times when he was feeling guilty or frustrated. He was still her sweet, strong George who had

promised that everything would be wonderful for them. It was just
this silly math that was confusing him.

Once it was clear that he wasn't coming back and the trailer
door had cooperated by allowing George his escape, Ruby took to
her bed and rolled up like a scared potato bug trying to make itself
too small to be stepped on. She ignored knocks at the door, and
the ringing of the phone did not move her to answer because she
knew it wasn't George. As with all the men who had come before
him, George had been her last hope. There was no life left to live
after George, and she couldn't go back to the one she had before
him. That one seemed far away—an insipid, useless routine.

Ruby decided she was going to die and she crawled into bed
to do it. She decided she would not eat or drink water or move
or even blink, unless of course she was crying. She cried so hard
that she thought the end would come quickly. She could feel her
insides ache as if a poison was running through them and the
skin over her temples pulsed until she thought the veins would
burst. Ruby was fairly certain, too, that hearts really could fly apart
because surely this was what it felt like.

She cuddled her cat, Dexter, close to her stomach, keeping a
hand buried in his soft belly fur, stroking him to comfort herself.
Dexter was content to lie with Ruby as long as she liked. He had
been rendered mentally retarded before he could remember he ever
wasn't, so, besides eating, drinking, and using his litter box, Ruby
was his world. She found baby kitten Dexter tied inside a plastic
bag in the trash bin out back of the Pioneer Café. He was down to
his last few squeaks when Ruby ripped open the bag and cradled
him against the fullness of her breasts, crying with rage and pity.

Unlike other cats, Dexter's gait had no grace. His back legs
turned in and he dragged them just a bit as he wound himself
throughout the house. He was clumsy, seldom able to make a triumphant jump into the bed without Ruby's helping hand. He was
not deft at, nor did he attempt to, capture cat toys. With a hypnotic
glaze to his eyes, he watched string dangle for as long as someone

dangled it. The vet said there was no question that Dexter's brain had been deprived of oxygen while inside the plastic bag, and more than likely he had also suffered a small stroke. Nothing to be done, said the vet. This was Dexter's life.

Ruby, too, thought this was her life, or what was left of it. George was the latest in a series of men who had broken her heart, and the pattern had been dawning on her for some time now.

Ruby's first husband was an Anglo who drove her from fairground to fairground where he rode bucking broncs and broke a lot of bones. After five years they had no permanent home and few plans to establish one, yet it was Ruby's husband who bought her a bus ticket home once the results came back that Ruby would never bear a child.

There had been a couple of good years with another man named Dennis, except that he broke things whenever he drank, and once put a bullet hole through the door of her car because she'd laughed at a joke shared between women that he wasn't supposed to hear.

Alfred stole her tip money while she slept and took off for Colorado, where he now worked an oil rig and had a pregnant girlfriend.

Michael took Valiums and slept all night and day, with no intention of ever getting a job in life.

Sergio had been the sweetest, always bringing her flowers for no reason, gifting a delicate gold bracelet after only a week of dating, giving her rides to and from work when her car broke down. But he began following her, even sitting in the Pioneer Café, sometimes throughout her whole shift, making her feel guilty if she smiled at her customers. He scowled if men admired Ruby's long black hair or stared into her face at the high curve of her cheekbones.

Ruby finally asked two of her brothers to talk to Sergio and make him go away. Her brothers found Sergio peeking into Ruby's window one night as she watched television and escorted him even farther into the dark. While one brother held Sergio's arms behind him, the other held a gun to his groin. The brother holding the gun assured Sergio that he was very understanding of how men who stalk women have an illness and should seek therapy. He understood, too, that therapy is expensive, pretty much impossible for the workingman to afford. He then pressed the gun harder into the front of Sergio's pants and said, "This is your therapy." Ruby's brother pulled the trigger, and although it was only a dry fire, Sergio screamed like a little girl and ran off into the dark, holding his crotch.

It was nothing short of a miracle. That night and forever, Sergio was cured of ever coming around Ruby again.

Ruby's brothers were able to rid her of bad choices; they could do nothing about her continuing to make them.

R uby wanted to be kissed as she lay dying. She wished she could call everyone she knew and, without explanation, say, "I'm leaving now; come kiss me good-bye."

She lay in her bed thinking of those she would call. She would call her brothers to say how much she appreciated their standing by her. They had been good brothers, she would tell them, the kind that all little girls wish they had.

She would, of course, call her best friend, JoAnne. They were two peas in a pod, they told each other. One year for Christmas, JoAnne even gave Ruby a ceramic pea pod meant for holding a kitchen sponge. Ruby found a tiny jewelry box in the shape of a pea pod, and JoAnne kept her most favored earrings inside of it. JoAnne was fearless, and she told the truth and didn't care who didn't like it. She was kind and forgiving, and she worked hard. The gift JoAnne had given to Ruby the most was laughter. Before she died, Ruby needed to tell these things to JoAnne.

She would call her older sister, Salina, and say she was sorry for the silly fights they'd had over the years. Ruby would

encourage her sister to kill her husband in his sleep because
the old bastard had it coming for being difficult to live with.
She might even offer to help her. Perhaps they could do it right
away, that night. Since she was going to die anyway in a couple
days, why not help her sister kill her husband?

Because it's a mortal sin! Ruby gasped aloud at her own
thoughts. You can't commit mortal sins just before you're going
to die. There isn't enough time to explain them away, to justify
them, and certainly not enough time to make up for them.

Salina would have to kill her husband on her own, thought
Ruby—but still she would call to offer encouragement for the plan.

Coming back to bed after brushing her teeth and seeking a
swallow of water, Ruby answered the phone without thinking.

"What are you doin'? ¿Qué pa-sooo, mujer? I been calling and
calling, ¿Qué haciendo? You're not at work—you're not answering
your phone—you're not calling me . . ."

Choking out the words, Ruby told her best friend about the
math, that George would never return, that she was just about to
call her because she was fairly certain this was the end because
she just couldn't take any more heartbreak, and why did life have
to be so complicated and filled with pain?

Lonely. That's the way she was meant to live out her days. This
was it, no more men, and she could see now that she was somehow
as defective as the men she chose, because why else would she
continue choosing them?

A long silence. A low, consoling groan of disbelief as JoAnne
reacted to George's desertion. Another long minute of no words
passing between the two women, Ruby weeping quietly on one
side of the line, her best friend listening to her in reverent com-
miseration on the other.

After another moment, Ruby's whimpers subsided to sniffles,
signaling JoAnne that it might be an open moment to respond
to her dear friend's grief. JoAnne knew it was important to say
just the right thing, something to comfort Ruby's aching heart,

mend her hope, and help her see that in spite of it all, a future remained for her. Clearing her throat, then, slowly, compassionately, assuming a soothing timbre when she finally spoke, JoAnne said, "Rúbea—you gotta quit accepting shit just to have something to hold in your hand."

He was the perfect man. He wasn't married. Ruby made sure this time. He had worked for the same oil company for years, a sure sign of stability and commitment. Good money, good benefits. Only drawback, he complained, was the traveling. He was tired of the traveling, living out of a pickup truck and motel rooms in three, four towns a year. Sometimes he discussed with Ruby his early retirement plans, just ten years off. He often looked longingly into Ruby's eyes when he said this.

He talked about his home state of New York. So much to see and do. Not like New Mexico, with boring desert everywhere you looked, litter stuck to the streets, and dead Indians along the highways. New Mexico was a ridiculous place to live, said Peter: backward, uneducated, full of alcoholics and unemployment. He couldn't wait to leave.

But, he said with a long sigh, you take the bad with the good, and his willingness to live uprooted in sometimes desolate places was why he got paid the money he did.

They had a wonderful time together. Trips to Old Town in Albuquerque for shopping and dinner. Another time to the flea market and then a concert. He took her to nice restaurants. No cafés—unless they were quaint and charming. No hamburgers.

He told her often that he thought her beautiful. But just as often, he added something that negated the compliment. She had a lovely figure, he commented, then added his observation that, unfortunately, all Hispanic women get round as they age, until they look like beach balls with appendages. He then laughed at the image he had created for himself.

Ruby recognized that along with the fun and the romance, Peter had his ways. But, everybody has their ways, she reasoned. Everyone has their small annoyances, certain ways of folding a towel, a routine they like to follow, that if they didn't do things a certain way, it made them feel undone. Ruby reminded herself that she too had her way of folding towels and admonished herself to be tolerant. They were, after all, still getting to know each other.

When Peter stayed at Ruby's trailer, he made sure to take all his things in the morning. He never left a toothbrush or a comb. The only evidence of his overnight visits was the trash he had discarded and the dishes he'd used in the sink. Ruby offered him a drawer and his own glass in the bathroom, but he quickly declined without platitudes or excuses.

When Ruby stayed with him, he always handed her the left-overs from the previous night's takeout dinner and made sure she had all her belongings, right down to the last bobby pin, when she left his motel. She once asked why he didn't sometimes keep the leftovers since there was a kitchenette with a microwave in his room, but his impatient scowl kept her from ever asking again.

After a couple of months Peter seemed tired, seldom possessing the energy to drive to Ruby's trailer park. She was the one to pack an overnight bag and make the twelve-mile trip in the opposite direction from her job, picking up dinner on the way. Still, she wasn't allowed to leave a change of clothing or a toothbrush. Everything came with her through the door; everything was piled into her arms when she left.

He said things that confused her. Peter called them "constructive suggestions" concerning the arrangement of her hair, her choice of friends, the furniture in her trailer house, the clothes she wore. His face took on mock surprise that she didn't catch on to things that were really quite obvious.

He admired that she had the courage to keep her hair long even though she was over thirty-five. Most women take on a haggard look with long hair after a certain age, Peter said. He liked her eye makeup, but admonished her that too much would make her look hard. Her choice of lipstick for a woman her age might be just a little too dark, he said.

As for her furniture, the best thing to do there was to throw out every stick and start over. Something less childish, what with the hand-sewn quilts on the bed, a white scrolled headboard and ruffled curtains at the kitchen window. He was amazed that the wingback chair was still able to sit atop its own legs, as old as it was. Had she inherited the weathered sideboard holding old plates and childish knickknacks?

But, he assured her, he loved her in spite of her bad taste and odd choices.

Peter's three months in New Mexico went by quickly. He talked of his next assignment, somewhere in Oklahoma, and looked forward to some time off. Ruby waited during these conversations for Peter to say something about her coming with him. She hoped he would tell her to sell her things and come to Oklahoma. Or, if not Oklahoma, surely he meant to take her to New York for his vacation time. Instead, he mused about seeing old friends and the things they would do together. Ruby was nowhere to be seen in these musings. She sat next to Peter at a restaurant or watching TV, answering in low tones that she was happy for him to have the chance to see his friends. She understood how he must miss his boyhood home. She had no idea what else to say, so she repeated phrases: You'll have fun doing that. You must be looking forward to that. That will be nice for you.

⸻ ◦ ⸻

L ike a fall you never saw coming, like a dodgeball in the face when you're six years old, and for whatever reason, perhaps because they loved Ruby, the gods conspired on that very day, at that very moment to give Ruby an epiphany. Ruby knew what an epiphany was but was raised to believe they were reserved only for saints. In one magnificent fleeting manifestation Ruby saw her life as it was, as it had been, how she had created it.

This time, Ruby did not take to her bed. Two weeks after Peter drove away from the trailer park promising a phone call that hadn't come, Ruby began reading all the self-help books she could find in the Farmington Library. She read about women who are enablers; women who lack self-esteem; women who seek punishment for crimes they had no hand in committing; women who are "fixers," meaning they gravitate to the broken-spirited, the emotionally needy, the insecure, and the unambitious to try to fix them—which, Ruby found out, was like buying parts to fix a Pinto; even if you could find the right parts, it's still a lemon.

She read about men who hate women and the women who love them. She didn't think she knew any men who actually hated women. Mostly she knew the ones who never had money and were crippled up in mind, body, or spirit. She read about men who sabotage relationships and men who can't commit. There were men who felt powerless, so they wielded power over those less powerful; men who had been abused so they became abusers, usually of women who had been abused and believed they deserved it.

By the time Ruby finished reading, she had seen herself in at least three of the books. She obviously fell into the nurturing doormat category. The ten-question tests at the end of each chapter in a book on self-esteem diagnosed her as definitely lacking in it. She didn't value herself enough, it said; therefore she was vulnerable to bad choices.

There was a clinic in Farmington. Freshly-papered doctors and psychology majors finishing higher degrees spent time there to gain experience. The fees were cheap, a sliding scale. Ruby decided to ask questions.

It had been a year since Peter rolled out of town without a backward glance, and much had changed. Ruby no longer allowed anyone to live with her. She refused to go to a bar on a date: the movies or dinner, perhaps a stroll down the mall; those were Ruby's conditions for a first date and a second. She now watched men, the way they treated others—waiters, clerks, people they ran into while having coffee at the diner. She watched the way they treated her and no longer privately provided excuses for behavior that confused her or hurt her feelings. She asked a lot of questions and became a good listener. She no longer accommodated the needs of others before or above her own. She now gave herself a say in who became her friend.

The true mettle of these changes would be tested when Ruby recognized the voice of the caller within the first syllable. Something akin to nausea swept through her body. She identified the nausea as the sort that comes with the adrenaline of terror. The terror, she later recognized, was a fear of what had already been, like the jitters hanging around after turning off a scary movie when you're in the house all alone. After the conversation with Peter ended, she would realize the fear was that she had not come far enough, had not evolved past the point of choosing the same bad situation again, a fear of herself.

She thought about hanging up the phone immediately. She and the therapist had discussed the possibilities of what she might do if Peter called and it was Ruby who suggested hanging up. The therapist gently wondered if perhaps it might be cathartic if Ruby took the opportunity to assert herself, perhaps tell him that while she took responsibility for choosing the relationship, she could now see what made her choose him, what had made her choose others like him in the past; and now that she knew, she would never choose that again.

Faced with the actual phone call, Ruby was struck mute and again the option of just hanging up was given preference. Besides, what was the use of attempting to talk about the past? As usual, he had the advantage of surprise, and although she'd gone over a thousand times in her mind what she would tell him at this moment, she knew the words would come out all wrong and that there would be something she would forget to say.

But then Peter's voice stammered and he sounded unsure of himself, and Ruby considered that perhaps he was calling to apologize. Perhaps somewhere in the unfolding conversation she would hear shame for promising to take her to see singer John Martyn as soon as the tour hit town, only to take another woman and then neglect to throw away the ticket stubs.

On the phone, a sweet resonance returned to his voice as he asked if she remembered the good times, the starry nights spent making love, the conversations over coffee as they sat in their underwear at daybreak. He told her no one had been able to fill the void. He'd just been running from woman to woman looking for what he'd already known with her. Did she remember he'd promised her a trip to New York to visit his boyhood stomping grounds, to show her the city, go to dinner, see Central Park? He wanted to make good on the promise now.

With the nausea subsiding a bit, Ruby asked rather flippantly why he had to move 2,000 miles back to New York and wait a year before calling to announce his epiphany. He explained that it was the very move that made him realize she was the one.

Could he send her a ticket, he asked. They could just see how it would go once she got there.

At first, Ruby wanted to scream no—no seeing how it would go. She already knew how it would go. Everything would seem wonderful until he fell into one of his so-called reminiscences. He would begin telling her about his former wife, the saint. The one who had rescued him from a life of indecision, the one with perfectly shaped breasts and the patience of Job. Over dinner, he would relate anecdotes of other women, providing too much detail, seeming not to notice how her face slowly slumped and she couldn't finish her food as he went on.

Oh, yes, thought Ruby as he begged her to accept the ticket to New York, she remembered his good times very well indeed.

But then something happened as he droned on about what fun they would have in New York, reminding her that she'd always wanted to see the Big Apple. Amongst all the cajoling and flattery, she felt something resembling the old insanity, and said yes—yes, she would come to New York.

Ruby hung up the phone, then smiled as the thought occurred to her that the therapist would not consider what she was about to do "healthy."

F ifteen minutes from touchdown, everyone was told to fasten their seat belts in preparation for landing. There was no need for Ruby to comply since she'd worn her belt throughout the journey, but the announcement prompted her to reach for the piece of carry-on luggage stashed beneath the seat in front of her. The butterflies churning in her belly since boarding the plane in Albuquerque now felt like moths beating against her insides. Delving into the satchel, she spied the strawberry-blond wig she'd picked out so carefully and pulled it from inside the bag, the same bag she used to pack for overnight stays with Peter. There was a newer bag at home she could have used, but bringing this one seemed poetic.

Feeling again inside the bag, she dug for a mirror and squeezed it between her knees, turning it until she stared into impish eyes and a mouth smiling with expectation. She found hairpins and began twisting her own black hair into a tight bun, then shook out the wig and adjusted it to her head. She apologized to her neighbor in the adjoining seat when her elbows invaded the woman's space, but made no explanation to assuage the perplexity settled on the woman's face.

As Ruby exited the plane, she adjusted a new pair of sun-glasses onto her nose. She'd made sure her traveling clothes were loose, not only for comfort but to conceal the exact shape of her figure. Coming to the end of the skyway, Ruby saw Peter standing near the door. He stood with anticipation in his eyes and a grocery-store bouquet of dyed daisies in his hand. Lowering her head, she pretended to look for something inside the bag hanging from her shoulder as she approached the spot where Peter stood passing the bouquet from one hand to the other. He kept his gaze on the door, paying little attention to the woman with short strawberry blonde hair as she brushed his shoulder in passing. From the corner of her eye, Ruby saw him do a quarter pivot to glance at the overnight bag bouncing against a hip as she walked farther into the crowd, but then he turned back to the gate entrance and squeezed the bouquet more tightly in his fist.

Walking out of the airport, Ruby flagged a taxi and told the driver she was staying at the American, near Central Park. She would be spending a week seeing the sights, she told the driver. Then she asked if he was able to suggest some good restaurants within walking distance of the hotel.

After All

Hortencia Alcón sat in a chair watching her husband die and pondered how she felt about it. He wasn't too young to die; seventy-two is a respectable age for dying, especially for a smoker, thought Hortencia. It means you've led a full life, at least as far as cramming the usual things into it: the wonders and disappointments of childhood, the lunacy and confusion of adolescence, the shocks and heartaches of marriage, the elation and anguish of children, working yourself stupid and ignoring the aches and pains until the eventual breakdown of the body made you pay attention to your age.

Yes, according to the list, Joe had led a full life.

Hortencia's seemingly dispassionate acceptance that her husband was dying didn't mean she wished him dead; Hortencia wasn't the sort of person to be glad about anyone's passing. The thoughts she pondered were concerned with how her life was going to be on her own. A half century is a long time to take care of someone, to work alongside him, to endure. Endure. That was how she felt about her life, and ultimately, about life in general.

Months ago, sitting in the doctor's office waiting for Joe's test results, Hortencia saw an article in *Reader's Digest* about resilience. It said that people who are resilient are more able to bounce back from worried times, lean times, disappointing times, even times of tragic loss. The article said also that people who are able to laugh recover more quickly from life's adversities.

How obvious and silly, thought Hortencia. *Everyone* ends up laughing. A person *had* to laugh—even if the laughter contained a trill of hysteria.

Hortencia had no idea if she were resilient. The article did not mention a scale of one to ten—the exact toll you might expect to pay for a given adversity and how much laughing you'd have to do to survive it. There was no meter, no psi gauge, not even a limit for the number of life's abhorrences you might endure before you were allowed to lose your mind and tell resilience to take a flying leap. Surely there was some end of expectation for being able to bounce back. Didn't resilience wear out at some point—like tires and rubber bands? Is a person expected to be resilient in all things? And exactly who *is* that resilient, if indeed someone like that exists?

The village idiot, laughed Hortencia to herself. He's pretty damned resilient. The man with the most money and the fewest friends—he can afford to be resilient. The alcoholic, who purposely and repeatedly renders himself senseless, so never fully endures anything. The priest: He's got no kids, somebody else pays all the bills, and he has God on his side.

Does getting up in the morning and doing what is expected of you day after day count as resilience—or endurance?

There was this to endure: Joe lying in a hospital bed, a sure thing that he would never leave it with his heart still beating. And the smell. There were the smells to endure. Joe didn't seem to mind if the nurses left him lying in his own filth for an hour after he'd filled the diaper. He simply lay in the disgusting waste, uncomplaining, seemingly unaware.

He doesn't have the energy to complain, Hortencia consoled herself. Maybe that's what happened. After a hard day's work, maybe Joe didn't have the energy to wipe the cow dung from his rubber boots before trudging across the clean, waxed floors. Or the energy to wash away the sweat and stench of the barn. Maybe there wasn't enough energy left at the end of the day to touch her long chestnut hair of years ago, or reach for her hand across the supper table in approval of the food she prepared day after day, year after year.

The nurse finally entered the room and changed Joe's diaper. Hortencia began taking deeper breaths and moved her chair closer to the hospital bed. She watched the nurse adjust mysterious tubes, take a reading from the blood pressure cuff attached to Joe's arm, and write down information on a clipboard. The nurse then patted Joe's hand and told his torpid face that he was doing fine.

Doing fine at what, wondered Hortencia. At dying? Was he right on schedule? Was his pulse slowing at the correct cadence, his body shutting down at the proper pace?

Hortencia watched the nurse straighten and tuck in the stark white sheets and allowed herself to wander through the thoughts of a young woman.

Joe had been dressed in white the night they met, his outfit matching those of the rest of the mariachis. A thin red bolo tie accented the dazzle of the starched white pants and long-sleeved ruffled shirt. He was a sight then, recalled Hortencia, a real sight for a young girl's eyes.

She had been surprised when the young man came up to her during the first intermission and wanted to know her name. He made her promise to meet him during the next intermission so they might talk again.

As they sat outside in hard-backed chairs, Joe told her of his dreams to have his own band and be famous like Herb Alpert . . . or start a dairy farm. He explained that he already had the land, passed from his great-grandfather straight down the paternal line to him. Right now he worked at the power plant and played in the band on weekends.

Hortencia revealed that she had lived on a farm all her life. Joe had smiled and taken her hand, and she had let him.

At the end of the dance, when they stood outside feeling awkward and yearning, Hortencia's brothers pulled up and told her that it was time to go home. Joe quickly asked if he might be the one to drive her home. He said he wanted to know exactly where she lived so he could find her again. A pact was swiftly sealed between Hortencia and her brothers that she would not tell about the liquor if they would not tell she had ridden alone with a man she'd just met—but, said her brothers, only if Joe and Hortencia got quickly into his car and followed them home—and there was a warning not to fall behind or turn off the main road.

———————

T he first baby came so soon after their marriage that Hortencia's own mother hinted disgrace at her daughter. Inside the church, Hortencia made a solemn oath to her mother that she had kept Joe at bay until their wedding night.

Joe, too, was surprised. He had hoped for a little more time. He continued to play in the band and resigned himself to working at the plant, but it often had layoffs that lasted months at a time, ensuring a cycle of desperation and then catch-up. Eventually, of course, Joe gave up the band. The time required for rehearsals, and the weekend engagements themselves was turned toward developing the dairy farm.

And so it began. One by one the children had come, the bills had come, the worries had come. When one worry had been resolved, another took its place, and the years passed without waiting for anyone to catch up.

After Joe gave up the band, the smell was what drove Hortencia from his bed. Her only defense was to separate herself from him. While the children were still small, she moved an extra bed into her husband's bedroom and slept apart from him. Every early morning in the dark while her husband slept, Hortencia crept to his bedside and slowly floated his filthy farm clothes into her arms and out to the laundry porch. When he awoke, Joe found clean clothing to put on and he dressed himself the same as if they had been the fetid clothes of yesterday. From a distance, the cleanliness of the clothes buffered the smell of him.

Hortencia tried all the inducements to get Joe to bathe more often. There were the coquettish invitations to join her in bathing. Later, she dangled physical closeness as his reward for bathing. When Joe got to an age when closeness mattered less than an early dinner and rest, Hortencia turned to ridicule, begging him to make himself presentable. Finally, the distance was so great that they became simply business partners, each counting on the other to fulfill the division of labor that all couples must delineate in order to survive.

Hortencia wondered if perhaps Joe tended to her during the flu and times of poor health simply because he needed her again once she was well—like nursing a cow. You don't spend money on a vet and stay up all night with a cow because you love it. You pray to God for the cow's recovery because it's worth money; you need it to continue producing to help you stay alive.

As the children walked into the mysteries of their own futures, Hortencia wondered if she too might walk away, walk toward something, some dream she'd had for herself. But there was no place to go. The energy and courage of youth had become the sedentary wisdom of old age and its need for security. Starting over now felt frightening, and the vision of effort overwhelming.

Instead, Hortencia claimed a room for her own. She set up a bedroom with ruffles, bright curtains, flowerpots, and potpourri. She continued to pilfer Joe's clothing from his bedroom floor, but with the children gone, her housework had lightened. Joe continued to work the farm as hard as ever.

Left together in the house, the conversations began tentatively, as one-sentence inquiries and short answers.

"Do you need your knives sharpened, Tencia?"

"Yes, Joe, they could use it. Thank you."

"No hay de qué," said Joe. "Nothing, it's nothing."

"Did Beto Archuleta come for his milk order?"

"Sí, sí, and he paid in advance for the month."

"Bueno."

"Sí. Sí. Bueno."

Joe asked her more often if there was anything she needed: a new dress for church; new gloves for her gardening; had she taken her blood pressure medicine?

One day, not realizing that Joe was still in the barn, Hortencia walked in to find him holding onto the top board of a stall and laboring to breathe. Silently, she picked up a bucket and began milking. "It's those damned cigarettes," said Hortencia. "They'll be the death of you."

Joe said nothing, but when Hortencia's bucket was filled, he took it from her and handed her another so she wouldn't have to get up or carry the heavy pail. "Gracias," Joe said.

"No hay de qué," answered Hortencia.

Now it had come to this. Sitting in a hospital room, watching someone she'd known for more than fifty years slowly suffocate. The shallow rise and fall of Joe's chest reminded her of a blacksmith's bellows laboring with faulty valves—unrelenting in purpose while negligible in its effect.

"Tencia." Joe's voice came from among the white sheets, and Hortencia leaned over him with her ear poised toward his mouth.

"¿Qué deseas, mi esposo? What is it, Joe?"

"Water," he managed to say. "Dame agua."

Holding the straw to Joe's lips and looking fully into his face, Hortencia recognized the young man who had driven her home the night of the dance. She settled onto the bed and wrapped her arms around his chest as tears rolled down the furrows of her face like water following the channels of a plowed field.

"Did you love me, Joe? Did you love me?"

How to Create an Accident

I t was an accident. Well, perhaps "accident" isn't exactly the word to describe what happened to baby Hilario, and yet maybe it is. After all, no one wanted it to happen, no one planned it—so that makes it an accident. On the other hand, the thing that happened, and that the people involved should have known better, makes it not an accident.

Rosa Armenta watched as her husband and brother-in-law played with her baby. She had already been told to stop fretting, to sit down and keep peeling her chile. They were grown men and knew what they were doing and they loved her latest-born as much as she did. Didn't she know that? They weren't going to let anything happen to him. Couldn't she see how much Hilario was enjoying their play? And indeed, the sound of Hilario's laughter was an afternoon concert as it echoed off the sandstone mesas of Pump Canyon.

The men continued to throw baby Hilario back and forth between them. Each time one man let go of him, sending him sailing through the air, the child chortled with delight. His father would say, "Mira, Hilario, you are flying," and Hilario's uncle caught him just beneath the armpits as the little body began to descend. Then his uncle would hold him up and whisper, "¿Quieres ir con tu padre, hijo? There, fly to him," and away flew little Hilario.

Rosa was almost able to stop the frolicking when Hilario's uncle caught him by just one arm. She had thrown down her bowl of roasted chile and screamed at the men, "Tontos, you will kill my baby!" Again Rosa was shushed and shamed back to her chair, where her hands ripped at the crackled skin of the roasted chile and her eyes darted back and forth as if watching a tennis match.

When baby Hilario flew through the air for the last time, his toothless grin was wide with the delight of innocence, his eyes shining with the wonder of weightlessness. When he fell to the ground, it was not his scream that filled the air of Pump Canyon; it was Rosa's.

Hilario's mouth lay soundless against the dirt, the left side of his face looking like dough bursting through the seam of a biscuit can. The eyes were now wide with shock, as were the eyes of all those who stood around him. Only Rosa dared touch him, hoping, as all mothers do, that her touch, the sound of her voice, was all he needed to make him whole again. But the damage was beyond a mother's magic.

And that is how an accident happens.

The Chariot

ilario Armenta turned into the El Nido Bar parking lot and inched into a front-door parking position, only to move the gearshift into reverse and idle the car backward. He had a favorite spot where it was impossible to park near him and nick the paint job on his 1964 Chevy Impala. Two cottonwood trees set back against the low ditch bank grew just far enough apart to allow only one car between them. Behind him, the ditch flowed thirty miles southwest from Navajo Dam to reach El Nido—water as cold as melted snow, the trough deep enough to nourish thirsty farmland for fifty miles more.

Soon that very parking place would be the setting for one of El Nido's most unusual misfortunes.

Hilario slowly opened the car door, careful to gauge the distance to the tree, and finally pushed it to its most open position. Even with the door at its widest, Hilario still had to take his time, first lifting out his left leg, then swinging the rest of himself out the door to stand erect while he captured his balance and caught his cadence.

Hilario's left hip moved as if cranked by a ratchet, as if some shade-tree mechanic had slapped in a used crankpin to keep the machinery going. When he threw his leg forward, the hip rotated out and up, as if it meant to overtake the height of his waist. Observers expected to hear the scraping of distressed metal escaping from beneath his skin as the jerry-rigged machinery struggled to operate the limb.

Hilario's hip, shattered by a childhood accident when he was too young to remember, had always been there. His life had always had a broken hip. Childhood was a series of casts and braces and operations. He could only wonder at what it was like to run, to walk quickly, or to rise from a chair without having to turn himself in a circle to get his balance. Bar stools were easier to dismount. He only had to lower his right leg to get himself steady, then drop the left leg and lock in his posture.

Most evenings after leaving his job at the San Juan Plant, Hilario drove to the El Nido Bar to talk with his best and only friend, Adolfo Flores. The two men commonly sat at the last elbow of the bar ordering one beer and then another, their conversations sedate and serious as they took turns paying Lily for the rounds. If one waved his money at Lily twice in a row, the other was insulted.

"Do you think I cannot pay!" Hilario might roar.

"Do ju tink I ahm a mon not to buy a drink for his compadre?" Adolfo growled back. The histrionic indignation commonly turned into a match of armwrestling and the loser was not allowed to pay. In truth, Adolfo would have won every match. He knew this, so he didn't.

The two men believed that they enjoyed talking politics, but in reality one took his cue from the other about what to believe and then they vied for establishing who felt more strongly about the issue.

It was the summer of 1973 and the newspapers rumbled with rumors that the Vietnam police action had finally run its course in the Asian theater of war. Hilario overheard two men in business suits talking on the steps of the community building in Farmington as he left from paying his electric bill and he now repeated in his own words to Adolfo the opinions of the men.

"It was all a mistake from the beginning, ¿que no?" said Hilario.

"Oh, jes, jes, dey make a mistaken from a day beginning," affirmed Adolfo.

"The French had already tried to tame the Vietnamese, but we did not learn from their mistakes," Hilario said.

"All a mistaken," said Adolfo.

"Vietnam was an unfortunate but necessary war," said Hilario.

"Notheng to be doan about such a theng," Adolfo lamented.

"War is war, and there have always been wars, and men have to fight them because there has always been something to fight about, ¿que no?"

"Sí, sí. Always esometheng," said Adolfo.

"Pero, ju know wah I ahm tinking, también?"

"¿Qué crees, amigo?" said Hilario, sipping his beer and encouraging his friend to express his opinion.

"I tink God shoult no leave so much a questions so we half to fight. Why no geeff each a dey peoples dey land where dey supposed to be and everybody estay dare?" Holding his hands as if illustrating the dimensions of each country, Adolfo parceled out the world on top of the bar. "Este es por los mexicanos, y este es por los alemanes, y el otro para los . . ."

Hilario nodded his head and tipped his bottle in Adolfo's direction to confirm that the statement was every bit as profound as Adolfo had meant it to be.

"Sí, sí, God is a mystery."

"Pero, at dey sane tine . . ." Adolfo raised his eyebrows and set his jaw while looking slantwise at Hilario. "At dey sane tine, amigo, wid-dout dey war, how dey coontries get greeeat laiders an' heroes, after all?"

"Sí, sí. Verdad. A man must be tested," said Hilario.

In other conversations Hilario and Adolfo left the fighting of war to the young, and its decisions to generals who had been tested, and talked quietly of boyhood. They savored memories of warm tortillas handed to them by mothers who fed their bellies with food and fed their souls with a kiss to the top of the head. Hilario said he now understood how tired his mother must have been. He now felt bad that he was the sort of child who cried at his mother's hem to pick him up, to carry him around, to pay attention only to him. His mind shuffled images of his mother directing the movements of eleven children getting ready for school; slapping tortillas onto a piece of flatiron heated on top of a wood stove; finding his mother asleep at the kitchen table while she waited for her chile to reach the exact moment of simmered perfection before turning off the flame and going to bed.

The men compared their childhood food and customs and found that many things were no different between one side of the border and the other. The bloodlines of both men were tied to New Spain. In the early 1800s the king of Spain began forgiving debts, even paying people to populate the Spanish possession in the Americas. Hilario's great grandfather rolled up his belongings and braved the voyage to Mexico, seeking opportunities as a blacksmith.

From New Spain, Hilario's great-grandfather traveled to the New Mexico Territory to cash in on offers of free land. His name appears among the first handful of deeds issued to those who settled El Nido: Jácquez, Candelaria, Manzanares, Archubeque, and Armenta.

Another family now held the deed to the land. Not even the outside horno where Hilario's mother had baked bread survived as a testament to the generations of Armentas who had lived in Pump Canyon.

Adolfo Flores had come to the United States packed inside a crate. His mother folded him neatly in among blankets going to the border town where his father's cousin sold Mexican wares. His family would join him in time, but until then he must do everything the cousin said. By never complaining, he would be helping to get his family to Los Estados Unidos muy pronto. His mother pinned money to the inside of his shirt and off went Adolfo inside a nailed crate that sat in a customs office for five hours until his father's cousin came to take possession. Adolfo was almost comatose from lying so still for so long between blankets with little air and no water. He had soiled himself and the smell was enough to keep the customs agents from breaking open the crate to verify the contents.

The cousin loaded the crate in the back of his pickup. Upon finding several ruined blankets, the cousin beat Adolfo and threatened that if he made his life difficult he would drop the boy at the border and let the agents figure out where he belonged.

Adolfo did not complain, but still it was months before his family made it over the border. Once together, Adolfo's father gathered the family and announced they would move farther north. The destination was El Nido, where the population spoke only Spanish and had no interest in sending people back over the border.

Hilario asked to hear the story many times, each time expressing his admiration for the bravery of Adolfo's family.

Such was the friendship of the two men that at times they confided regrets.

"I weesh I geef my wife more tangs," said Adolfo. "She neber complain, pero her life shoult half bean bedder. So beauteeful, my wife. La vida I geef her was neber easy," said Adolfo.

At these times Hilario often put his arm around his friend's shoulder and assured Adolfo that he was a great man, a superior man, a man of honesty and great strength, a man who had done his best throughout his life.

The two friends talked of life itself—the mystery of it—the point—the ongoing shock of what life requires sometimes spreading across their faces until neither could explain or say anything more, and they sat in the consoling silence of comrades—waiting for the paralysis to wear off before they were able to begin talking again.

Adolfo spoke of the death of his wife in short sentences, as if he were still piecing together exactly what had happened, looking for the exact thing, the exact moment when one thing might have been done differently to prevent her illness.

To his friend, Adolfo let it show what the event had done to him, the helplessness when a thing cannot be undone. That one shock amongst all the many that life delivers—the one you didn't see coming, the one you didn't deserve.

Such losses, Adolfo believed, chisel at the mind's balance. Adolfo teetered between the wisdom of accepting life as a risk, and the ordinary madness that tires the mind to its knees until it can't get up again.

Hilario regretted the loneliness of never marrying; he was ashamed that he had ended up so lonely, so vulnerable. He was afraid of losing Adolfo. What if something happened to his only friend? He was ashamed that he lived apprehensively in the world. He was a cripple who led a fearful life with little to show for it.

Except his car.

Hilario's Chevy Impala was his one possession of worth. When he drove it, people smiled at him. Men gave him a thumbs-up and young women looked his way until they assessed his age and the worn collar of his coat. Still, they looked.

The car was candied-apple red, with chrome wire rims. Inside was red and white tuck 'n' roll done at a shop just across the Texas border in Juárez. Hilario won the car in a lottery held to raise money for baseball equipment at El Nido Elementary School. Sheriff Maximillan Venezuela had donated the treasure of his twenties to the cause.

Hilario bought the ticket at the Four Queens Bar and liquor store in Bloomfield—not understanding what it was for—and put it in his wallet. Several months later he stood in line to buy his six-pack behind two men who were wondering out loud why no one had claimed the car.

"Probably some guy from outta town," remarked one. "Ol' Jorge Serna probably had it in his one suit when they buried him," laughed the other.

It was then that Hilario remembered the ticket and grappled for his wallet. He couldn't allow himself to believe it might be true, but tore at the contents of his wallet anyway. And there it was, the ticket was still there. Checking the ticket, Hilario squinted at the numbers on the wall and back down at those he held in his hand. He blinked as if to focus his eyes and moved his lips as he read the numbers again.

They matched. He couldn't believe it. They matched.

It didn't matter that the car was used. It had a brand-new paint job and a knob of red crystal at the end of the gearshift. Two naked women made of chrome, sitting stiff-backed and submissive while the wind blew their long hair away from their bodies, held the license plate.

Now no one could say he had nothing to show for his life. Winning the car meant he was lucky. The car made him special. It meant the saints were rewarding him for something good he had done.

Sometimes after recovering from the silences shared with his friend, and often coupled with getting too drunk, Hilario made Adolfo promise that he and the car would be buried together. "It would make the most beautiful of coffins, ¿que no?"

"Sí, sí, dey best of coffins," Adolfo had answered. "Pero, let us not espeak of death when der is so much beer to drink."

"Yes, yes, but do you promise?"

Adolfo unfailingly clutched his friend by the shoulder and promised, often with tears in his eyes, that Hilario and the Chevy would go through eternity together.

Enough people overheard the extracted promise that it soon became a joke around the bar when the two men were not there. Beto Archuleta said that anyone was welcome to bury his car right now, right after he borrowed a .357 from ol' man Rosario and shot it through the engine. Ol' man Rosario said he preferred that his wife be the one to get buried along with his car. Beany Moreno said she wanted a pink Cadillac to serve as her casket, but then laughed and said that with her luck she'd count herself fortunate to get buried in a burned-out Pinto.

Bubbles De La Cruz said he wanted a Crown Victoria—not as a casket, but as a home. He ruminated aloud that a Crown Victoria would be a mansion with the seats removed. Of course, only old people drove such cars and old people rarely got into car accidents serious enough for the car to end up in Freddie's junkyard—unless the car was hit by a semi, and then it was no good anyway because the car would be smashed into only one room and he already had his pick of vehicles with only one room.

Lily said she wanted back the jeep she'd bought for her worthless ex-husband—not to be buried in, but to dowse with gasoline and put a match to it in front of him, then watch him run around in hysterics trying to put out the fire and screaming like a little girl.

———❖———

T hat Saturday had been a fine night for drinking and talking too loud at the bar. Men had been paid the day before and the dance hall opened up for a wedding celebration. Everyone is welcome at a wedding dance. It's the custom. A hall is rented for the reception, a band is hired, and the doors are thrown open for all to enjoy. It cost nothing to engage the El Nido Dance Hall; the owners were satisfied to collect the extra revenue from the uncommon swell of customers. The people drank and danced until the band quit, and the band played until people stopped sending drinks.

Adolfo and Hilario spent considerable time that night recalling women from the past, women who became more beautiful with each telling. Adolfo described women he had seen on the streets of Farmington when he was a young man, then embroidered them into stories of moonlit evenings spent charming these women into falling helplessly into his arms and allowing him to have his way with them. Of course, since these women's virtue had been surrendered without demand of marriage, Adolfo could no longer consider any of them someone he might make his wife, and he abandoned them to men who accepted less than the sort of woman he required.

His María, his sweet, virtuous María; he knew when she did not succumb to the hypnosis of his charm that she was the one.

She saved herself for their wedding night, Adolfo proudly disclosed to Hilario.

With little experience of his own, Hilario described women he'd seen on Telemundo soap operas. He provided explanations to Adolfo for why he had never married any of these women: one died tragically at a young age, another was seduced by city lights and ran off to Albuquerque, another was carrying another man's child, and yet another wanted him only for his money.

After many beers, closing time came for Hilario around eleven o'clock. That was the time Adolfo said he put Hilario into his car to sleep it off. He'd rolled down the windows a bit to make sure Hilario had air on the warm summer night, but left them up far enough and locked the doors so that no one was able to play pranks on his sleeping friend. Hilario's keys were placed in his pocket for whenever he came out of his coma. It was a chain of events that had happened many times before.

No one would have thought, no one could have imagined, no one heard a thing.

The revelers had danced until two. They wore confetti in their hair, toasted the bride and groom (long since departed) with bottles of beer, and finally helped each other to their cars and drove cautiously home. Some passed near Hilario's car as they made their way to their own. A few tapped on the glass to bid him a boisterous good night or peered inside to get a good laugh at Hilario sleeping with his head tilted back against the seat and his mouth open.

"He's going to catch flies with that mouth," they guffawed.

"Or a whole bullfrog with the fly already inside," added someone, believing himself very funny. Adolfo stopped too, checking the doors, kicking the tires, contenting himself that his friend was safe. Then he walked home to his small dwelling just across the El Nido highway and fell asleep without taking off his clothes.

The next morning was like so many high-desert mornings—cool, the air fresh, as if laundered the night before and set out to dry as the day got progressively warmer. Adolfo rose early, as was his custom. Even with a lethargic body and an achy head, he did not like missing the cool mornings. He made his strong cowboy coffee and took it outside where he sat under a willow tree to observe small creatures make their living. He watched ants carry ten times their weight in unidentifiable material; beetles nosed through the dirt as if on a mission; dragonflies buzzed cattails growing along the ditch bank. His eyes followed the ditch running in front of his dwelling, crossing under the highway and continuing along in front of the El Nido Bar. He looked across the highway toward the El Nido Bar and at first glance saw what he expected to see—Hilario's car gone from its parking place between the trees in front of the ditch. He imagined his friend awakening in the dark hour just before dawn and driving himself home to rest more comfortably. But a second glance riveted his eyes to something incongruous to the scenery he knew so well.

There was something shiny sticking out of the eight-foot-deep ditch, sticking right out of the middle of it.

Investigating incongruous sightings was a pastime in El Nido, so Adolfo put down his coffee cup, adjusted the sweat-stained fedora to ride more securely on his temples, and sauntered toward the glimmering object that had no business being where it was.

As Adolfo got closer, he thought he could make out what the object was, but his mind refused to believe him. It was a bumper, the front bumper of a car sticking straight out of the middle of the El Nido ditch like a missile set for launch. Adolfo began to laugh, thinking Beto Archuleta had finally shoved the lemon he'd been driving for so long into the ditch. He stopped laughing when he got close enough to see the top of the hood and front fenders protruding from the water. The car below the water was red—candied-apple red.

D eath had come for Hilario dressed in his mother's clothing. She held a warm towel and surrounded him with it as she drew him from his bath. He shivered for a moment before his mother wrapped him up and hugged him to her breast. He was five years old and his mother had all her teeth and she didn't look tired. She had time to hold him for his very own moment, as many moments as he wanted, while he jabbered to her everything his little-boy mind had been thinking that day.

For Adolfo, Hilario's death came layered in its common garb, the dreary drab of despair, the ink-black of loss that never bleaches lighter no matter how long it's been scrubbed with time. Another thing that could not be undone.

It was enough to break your heart hearing the story of how Adolfo had jumped into the water trying to break a window, open a door—and that was after he'd already jumped onto the front bumper, pulling at it uselessly with his bare hands, screaming, "Hilario, Hilario! ¡Espérame, compadre! Wait for me!"

Ol' man Rosario wandered among the emergency vehicles and the small crowd explaining what he believed to be the scenario leading Hilario to his death.

"It doesn't take a rocket scientist to figure out what happened," proffered Rosario. "The poor bastard woke up wanting to go home. Fished his keys out of his pocket. Put her in reverse and forgot to stop."

He repeated this as each new person joined the vigil waiting for Hilario's car to be wrenched from the water.

The car was finally secured to the tow truck and the driver was set to take it one way while Hilario's body was destined for another. Adolfo planned to follow the body, but not before asking Beto Archuleta if he would tell the driver to tow the car onto his land until they figured out what to do with it.

Beto did not know there was a decision to be made. With Hilario dead and the car ruined by water, Freddie Montalvo's wrecking yard ought to be given the car as payment for pulling it out of the ditch.

As much sense as that made, Adolfo said Hilario's car was not going to any wrecking yard, and if Beto wouldn't save him the trouble and expense of getting the car out of hock and back to El Nido, he would find another way. He would find the money somewhere, some way, somehow, and, given the courage from God to carry on, there would come a miracle that would help him in his quest, and he knew Hilario was watching them from above as they stood beside the watery site of his death, and Adolfo wasn't sure where he'd get the strength or the money, but as Hilario's only friend . . . until Beto raised his hands in surrender and said, "All right, all right, Adolfo, the damned car can live at my place for a while."

Then, after a quick calculation of how long his brother-in-law had left a '58 Edsel inside his barn with flat tires and a transmission on the ground, Beto added, "Thirty days, Aldolfo. Thirty days. Or I start parting out the car myself."

In New Mexico it's possible to get permission to bury a body on your own land. Neither Hilario nor Adolfo owned any land, and asking permission to dig a grave on someone else's property proved troublesome. A lot of people who knew Hilario did indeed have land, but it gave them something to think about when it came to volunteering a plot big enough to bury a car with a body inside. People became sort of superstitious about the whole thing, as if maybe Hilario was going to suddenly come driving out of the ground in the middle of the night and give the whole family heart failure.

People wanted to help; it took every fiber in them to say no to Adolfo when he stood before them weeping, holding the fedora and twisting the brim, asking for something that wasn't for himself at all.

Beto Archuleta was the one who finally made it clear to Adolfo. As cruel as it sounded, he said, "Dammit, Adolfo, this makes about as much sense as a soup sandwich. I wasn't the one who promised him, so quit asking me. And nobody else wants to bury him either, so quit asking *them*, too."

The bare brass of his own words made Beto feel sorry. So, with a hand on Adolfo's shoulder, Beto added that if Adolfo found some place to bury Hilario, he'd find a backhoe and dig the grave for nothing.

In the meantime, the funeral home had done what they do with dead bodies. Hilario was eviscerated, embalmed, and enameled, then camouflaged in a Sunday suit. Adolfo told the mortician to be sure to put a smile on Hilario's face. The mortician answered that his job was to make people look natural, as if asleep, and people don't have smiles when they sleep. Adolfo answered back, "Suntines dey do. When dey dream about suntheng good."

Everything was set for the display and mourning of Hilario Armenta—except there was no interment site. The mortician, annoyed at waiting for someone to make a decision, put Hilario in cold storage.

After Beto set him straight, Adolfo was ashamed of himself for not thinking of it sooner. Who needed to own land to bury Hilario when the whole state was full of vacant, often unwanted, land? What was wrong with just picking a site out in the middle of nowhere and digging a hole?

There was a lot wrong with that, according to the State of New Mexico, and the mortician wasn't releasing a body that had nowhere to go. People can't just go around digging holes and planting cars with bodies in them. And just what did Adolfo think the mortician was supposed to enter into the books concerning the interment location of one Hilario Martínez Alejandro Fidel Armenta: "Eight miles west on the Aztec Highway, turn left onto oil field road 97, look for a clump of cottonwood trees off the old sheep trail at Navajo Springs Mesa, and not too far from the burnt stump is a grave big enough to hold a car."

Oh, sure, said the mortician, that would look just great written in his ledger.

Adolfo went back to Beto. OK, he said, I'm not asking you to bury Hilario on your land, but will you lie and say you will?

Nobody was ever sure exactly how Adolfo talked Beto into it, but after Hilario had been in the refrigerator for about a week, Beto signed the papers saying he was a distant cousin and that he was going to take Hilario to his place for burial. The whole thing was a lie, of course; Beto and Hilario shared about as much blood as a raccoon with a cat, but the funeral home owner was so anxious to be rid of Hilario that he too lied to the county office, saying he'd known the men for years and Hilario and Beto were indeed cousins. So then the woman at the county office lied and stamped the papers because she and the funeral man's wife were good friends, saying she'd seen proof of blood relation.

After a day of everybody lying to everybody else, all of them knowing they were lying to each other, and all of them swearing to it, the pine box with Hilario's body inside was loaded into the back of a borrowed pickup truck.

Adolfo felt he had chosen the perfect place to bury Hilario. The road called El Cañón de Tierra Feliz, leading north out of El Nido, dead-ends into the Aztec Highway. From there, it's a right turn and up about a mile. Then it's a left onto a dirt road that turns back on itself headed west. It looks like a thousand other oil field roads leading off into nowhere, but all of El Nido knows it's the way to the old sheep camp. Because there is water, it's been used for more than 150 years as the halfway stop for herders taking sheep to the Aztec sale barn. The dirt road meanders for a good four miles through sagebrush and crossing narrow arroyos until the mirage of a mesa shimmers in the distance. It's as if the mesa is a phantom that chooses to materialize when there is some living thing passing by in need of a drink of water, then shimmers back into the ground after the passerby has drunk his fill. The water comes from inside the stone mesa, filtered through rock and steadily dripping clear, clean, and cold into a small pool.

The trickling runoff feeds giant oak trees and lush native grass. An adobe shack outfitted with an ancient cast-iron stove and a teetery oak table sags against the mesa. Anyone is welcome to use it for the night.

This was the place where Adolfo wanted Hilario to rest. The sun would wake him in the morning. The clear water would wash and nourish him; the scenery would keep him serene. He would get company several times a year when the sheep men came with their flocks. Hilario would feel like a boy again when the teenagers came every year after graduation, bringing their bottles and raucous laughter. Watching them, he would forgive himself for not knowing the things he had mistakenly expected from himself in youth.

The mesa would watch over him, sending cool breezes from the oak trees in summer and breaking the blowing snow in winter.

When Beto rode up on the backhoe, Adolfo right behind him towing the Chevy Impala and toting Hilario's casket in the back of the borrowed pickup, there was a little crowd already assembled. Beany was there holding flowers and wearing a white lace dress and tennis shoes. Ol' man Rosario was there holding a couple of bottles. Lily was there, believing that serving countless drinks to a person means you knew them well. Bubbles was there, hoping the funeral needed his help. He had written an eight-page eulogy, but after turning out his pockets, he couldn't find it.

The pine box holding Hilario, of course, would not fit into the Chevy, so Adolfo picked up his friend and placed him behind the wheel. It was where he really wanted to be. Then Adolfo placed autographed pictures of Telemundo soap opera stars in the glove box.

It wasn't much of a ceremony, mostly Adolfo crying piteously and repeating, "Mi compadre, my freend. Vaya con Dios, mi amigo," while everybody gave him hugs and said nice or funny things they remembered about Hilario. Rosario emptied one of the bottles into the massive grave to consecrate the ground, he said, and passed the other one around. Lily thought it peculiar to commemorate Hilario's death with the very thing that had killed him, but said nothing and took a symbolic swig from the bottle as it made its round.

Hilario leaned back against the seat with his eyes closed, his lips sewn into a slight smile, dreaming of a dance with a big-chested Mexicana who whispered love into his ear.

The Rules of Murder

I n the 1970s El Nido had unwritten laws more rigidly observed that any judicial system could ever hope to enforce. It was a place of common sense and extenuating circumstances, with the circumstances extending further for some than for others.

There was a time when perpetrating a crime while drunk was allowed as a mitigating circumstance that should be weighed when presenting a defense—except of course in the case of actually being drunk. If you did something while drunk that you wouldn't ordinarily do when you weren't drunk, then it could be reasoned that you were out of your mind and therefore not in complete possession of your reasoning abilities, and so not fully responsible.

Jesús Montalvo used the fine line between *being* drunk and doing something while drunk to his best advantage, telling the judge that if he hadn't been drunk he would have known better than to sing and throw rocks at the house of the widow Guzmán, finally breaking a window, scaring her half to death, and prompting her to fire off both barrels of a twenty-gauge, further disturbing the sleep of half the town. He said he shouldn't be held accountable for something he did while out of his mind with drink, not to mention the intoxication and inseparable madness that inevitably accompanies love.

Judge Musgrove laughed until he had to excuse himself from the bench, then returned and suspended a 10-day sentence if Jesús promised not to sing after ten o'clock on city streets—and, if the widow Guzmán required it, he must leave her property immediately upon being asked.

If two men are fighting over something and both are so stubborn that neither one wants to give an inch, well then, it's almost inevitable that one of them is going to get hurt—or in the case of Raúl Pacheco, dead.

Some said Joaquín Ramírez "should never have diverted so much as a trickle of Raúl Pacheco's water because it was the same as stealing no matter how you looked at it." Others said, "Raúl always was a stingy son-of-a-goat with his neighbors and it didn't matter how many acres he put into production, he'd still have enough water rights to irrigate half of New Mexico."

The jury must have decided that being stingy was more heinous than committing murder because Joaquín got only three years for shooting Raúl. To be fair, though, they did tack on an extra year since Raúl was shot in the back.

Lester Trujillo got just six months for shooting his wife squarely between the eyes. Personality plays a big part in whether you will be missed by the community. To most people the only wonder was why it took Lester so many years to shoot his wife. Everyone knew Esther was hard to get along with. She was known as a lazy woman who didn't take care of her husband and made his life miserable by complaining every time he was within listening distance.

After working in the field all day, Lester walked into his two-room house and there sat Esther, still wearing her morning robe and no dinner made, and the first thing she said was, "Give me a cigarette."

Lester did not hand her a cigarette; he didn't acknowledge Esther at all. He simply passed on by the couch and went into the bedroom, where he checked to see that at least one bullet was in the .38 special. Then Lester came out of the bedroom and stood in front of Esther. She waved an angry arm and blustered that he didn't have to be so sullen all the time, and why couldn't he see that he could certainly make her life a little nicer by being easier to get along with, thank you very much.

Lester answered yes, he could see that, and put the gun to Esther's forehead. Through unblinking eyes, Esther watched her husband leave the house and close the door behind him. He went to the El Nido Bar to use the pay phone and waited there until Sheriff Max arrived and they both drove back up Largo Canyon. Sheriff Max later described to his wife, Perlita, what had transpired at the Trujillo household: Esther looked as she always did—just sitting on the couch, wearing a squalid housecoat and crumpled hair. He said that of course "you had to discount the blackened hole taking up about an inch of her forehead," but other than that, she looked pretty much the same as she always had.

The rules for infidelity for men and women were not the same. If a man found his wife in bed with another man he had the right to shoot them both, as long as he did it right there on the spot. If he didn't do it right then, it sort of ruined his defense of an "irresistible impulse," which was a very popular and successful one. If he was drunk at the time as well, acquittal was a shoo-in.

If a man only suspected his wife of cheating, he had the right to beat her. Of course, if she was innocent, she had the right to hit him back with the nearest black-bottomed pot.

If a woman found her husband in bed with another woman, she was entitled only to rip every hair out of the other woman's head, then kick her husband out of the house for a respectable amount of time to prove to the neighbors that she had her pride. She also had the right to throw his clothes out the front door and drive a tractor over them before or after she hocked his guns at the Honest Deal Pawnshop. Naturally, the woman had the right to threaten divorce—but no one would believe her, particularly not the husband.

If a woman only suspected her husband of cheating, she was allowed to go through his wallet while he was in the shower, search his clothing for evidence, and peek inside the swinging doors of a bar in an attempt to catch him in the act. At no time was she allowed to shoot her husband for cheating or for any other domestic crime when it came right down to it, because it was understood among the Hispanic community that women stayed—no matter what.

Sheriff Max often summed up women's lot in life the same way he accepted most things. For Max, the division of labor should have been a simple matter and easily determined according to gender.

"A woman ought to just expect that her husband is going to give her trouble once in a while—same as a farmer should expect drought, vermin, or aggravation from his mule. It's nature," said Max. "A woman inherits the burden of caring for children because of her body. And a woman needs a man to help her raise her children, so she takes him on too. These women's libbers can't change nature."

In 1978, Sheriff Max did not expect that Maggie Serna would go against the nature of El Nido and do what its women were not allowed to do.

The Monster Outside the Door

J orge Serna had never cheated on his wife. Not that he had any compunctions about cheating, but mainly it was because when he was in a bar, he was surly and brooding and had little interest in anyone besides himself. Not that Maggie would have cared if he cheated. Well, perhaps just a little—in the past—the inaccessible past, when Jorge told Maggie she was pretty, that she would be his whole universe if she consented to marriage. In her youth her insides would have twisted up to near explosion at the thought of Jorge being with another girl. Then, after some years and the first few children, if Jorge showed attention toward another woman, Maggie felt only embarrassment.

But Jorge hadn't cheated, and that's not why Maggie shot him.

Jorge didn't know he was a monster. He didn't know what he was, or what anyone else was, for that matter. Words like "father" or "husband" or "friend" were just words to identify things to him, much like "coffee mug" or "pickup truck." "Husband" meant he was married in the eyes of the law and the Catholic Church; "father" meant his wife had borne children and he had been the cause of it. He didn't seem to know that "father" meant reassuring children that the shapes in the dark couldn't harm them; that going to the elementary school Halloween party made them proud to have parents and feel that they had a right to be part of the world. And he didn't know that "husband" meant kissing your wife because there were always fresh tortillas inside a flour-sack towel on the counter, or that year after year she made sure you had clean socks and toothpaste in the bathroom. He couldn't imagine anyone loving him. He married and had children because it was what people did. He didn't know why he'd done those things any more than he knew why he did the other things he did. He didn't know why his wife wept while standing at the kitchen sink looking out the window. He never questioned why a visible, involuntary convulsion went through his wife's body when a door slammed or why his children hid from him when he was home. Jorge thought all families lived that way.

If he went with his family to a gathering at someone's home, he was sure the laughter stopped as soon as the company departed, the children slinking behind chairs with stones for eyes, the wife turning mute while performing chores without interest or energy. He was sure that all men bellowed commands and all women followed them with heads lowered into their chests.

They made him do it—drove him to it. They asked for it. She could deny it all she wanted, but he had seen the glances between his wife and her second cousin at a funeral the month before. They had even embraced in front of everyone after the services were over, shaming him, embarrassing him that she allowed another man to know the comfort of her breasts. And he knew why his wife volunteered to clean the church once a month. She was meeting someone in the recreation room. They would be able to lock the doors from the inside and stay as long as they wanted. He knew.

And another thing: Where did all his money go—his children in secondhand coats and his wife serving beans and lamb chile and tortillas every day of their lives? Jorge had managed to keep his job at the coal plant all these years and yet they never seemed to live better than the years before.

There were so many children. Someone was always crying. What was so hard about giving some peace and quiet to the person who put food into your mouth? Couldn't they see he was tired after working all day—he deserved to drink a little something so he could relax. He deserved a little respect from the people he supported. Instead, he got crying children, the living room too crowded for him to sit in comfort, always having to wait to use the outhouse.

Sometimes the beer in his bladder gave him no choice but to step outside into the dark. More than once he called to his wife to help him get his pants back up to his waist. She always took her time about coming to help him too. And if she dared look annoyed, he let her have it. He let her know, all right.

Was it any wonder he had to leave his own home to find some peace? They meant to do it—always testing him. Always taking their time, always in the way, never respecting him the way they should, never listening to him. Always making him feel so lonely.

Those chosen for a beating from among the seven children varied from one tirade to the next depending on who was awake or closest. Maggie, however, was never spared.

If she was asleep when he came in, she was pinched or punched awake and ordered to pour his liquor while making his breakfast. The breakfast had to include tortillas made from fresh dough while Maggie listened to Jorge rail about his life and curse the lives of his family.

Between turning tortillas, Maggie filled Jorge's glass, hoping to bring him quickly to passing out. Someone told her of a thing called alcohol poisoning, but she didn't believe it. Jorge seemed able to drink all she poured.

Sometimes he fell face-first into the eggs and chile, and Maggie would have to clean him up before putting him to bed. Many years before, she tried leaving him to snort his sleep through the food left in front of him, but morning brought another beating, delivered by a madman with dried yolk on his face because she had failed to take care of him.

I t wasn't obviously clear to Sheriff Max what had finally pushed Maggie into deciding that her husband would not enter his four-room home again. He knew only that the decision must have been made because her children had helped her barricade the doors, usually left unlocked (indeed, had no keys), with the shabby sofa and the heavy chiffonier that held the underwear of all seven children.

The children were told that they were all gathered in the living room to have a slumber party. They had never heard of a slumber party, and they weren't quite sure why all of them sleeping in the living room made it a slumber party when all of them sleeping in the bedroom wasn't. But the confusion was a wisp of wonder that passed quickly through their minds and soon all the children believed that being in a living room in your pajamas really did make it a party. When asked why they'd had to move furniture, Maggie was rescued by her own hesitation.

"To keep out the monsters while we have our party, silly-head," said her youngest child. And Maggie instantly agreed that keeping out monsters was indeed the very reason.

There was popcorn and penny candy and hot chocolate while each child took a turn telling their scariest ghost story or made shadows on the wall with their hands. The children were wild with freedom, allowed to bounce on furniture, spill their treats without reprimand, and laugh as loudly as their voices would carry.

Earlier in the day, out of the sight of the children, Maggie's fifteen-year-old son, Felipe, had loaded both barrels of the shotgun and shown his mother how to brace it against her shoulder. All the while, he kept asking if perhaps he should be the one to hold the gun since his mother had no experience with such things.

Maggie had been adamant. No child should point a gun at a parent; no child should show such disrespect—and perhaps it would not be necessary to actually point the gun at Jorge; she would yell through the door that she had the gun and that would be enough to make him go away. If she had to, she would pull the trigger once to let Jorge know she meant business. Then, Maggie promised her son, as shameful as it was, she would go into town the next day and "ask for the papers that make a divorce."

Pallets lay this way and that in the living room and when the hour grew late, Felipe made the children snuggle into their blankets while he told stories of brave children setting off in splendid ships to discover new lands. Maggie sat in a chair with its back against a wall, a loaded twelve-gauge wrapped inside a quilt resting against the wall behind her.

The stories were so serene, so filled with rocking oceans and beautiful promises that Maggie herself fell asleep in her chair, forgetting to listen for the first twist of the knob.

While his family slept, Felipe lined up everyone's shoes near the door. He leaned behind his mother's chair and undressed the shotgun from its cover and left it where it was.

A bare whisper of smoke puffed out of the stone chimney and a rainbow of blankets, thrown over sun-streaked curtains, hung in the windows. Not a single careless fold allowed the slightest sliver of light to stream out into the night. The Serna house crouched and drew itself inward like a shivering animal trying to stay warm and safe. All life, inside and out, seemed burrowed in—waiting.

———— ◆ ————

W hen Jorge turned the door handle and met with resistance, he cursed the March wind for freezing the door shut and heaved himself harder against it. His curses became familiar bellows as he continued to throw his shoulder into the door, calling his wife's name, commanding her to come and help him.

With the first blow to the door, Maggie flew out of the chair and stood in the middle of the room, her heart pounding, her hands twisting and clawing at each other as if trying desperately to remember what she was supposed to be doing with them at this moment. Her first inclination was to obey her husband, to let him in, to stop the roaring. Had it not been for Felipe handing her the gun, then standing behind her, buttressing her stance, she might have done that very thing and everything would have gone on as it always had.

The children lying on their pallets pulled the covers over their heads, trying to muffle the sound of madness raging outside the door.

The gun was too heavy for Maggie's hands and the barrel wavered around the room, aiming at the ceiling, then dipping toward the children, then directed in a straight but quivering line.

"Tell him to go away, Mother," Felipe whispered, and Maggie did as she was told.

"Vete de aquí, Jorge. You cannot come into this house tonight."

"¿Vete de aquí?" screamed Jorge through the door. "You are telling me to go from my own home! I should kill you!"

Then a sound more terrifying than the rage enveloped the house: the sound of silence.

Maggie and her son stood with the gun pointed at the front door until the crash of shattering glass coming from another part of the house whirled them around to stare at the black opening leading into the back rooms. Within one long second Jorge stood before them, his face warped into an abstraction of human features. He looked at the gun, then at his wife, then at his son, and began to laugh.

The gun slipped several inches from the crook of Maggie's shoulder, resting limply beside a breast, and Felipe reached around his mother to put it back. His hand stretched along the butt until it found the safety and a deft finger clicked it off.

"So you will kill me. You and this skinny boy." Jorge spat the words as if they were bile. He faked a lunge at his wife and son and laughed again when they jerked back a step.

"Go away, Jorge," pleaded Maggie softly. "Go away—and live."

Felipe's hand traveled along the gun until he felt his mother's hand and found the curl of her index finger over the trigger. Then he slipped his own finger over hers.

"Puta," screamed Jorge, "you are too stupid to shoot the devil before you!" And he raised his fist.

Maggie felt her finger pull back on the trigger. She watched Jorge's chest explode before her and felt drops of blood and small pieces of flesh pelting her face and catching in her hair.

The gun clattered onto worn linoleum, and Maggie herself might have slumped to the floor had her son not caught her beneath the arms and set her back into the chair where earlier she had dreamt of sunsets and safe harbors. Felipe then retrieved the gun, removed the unused shell from the second barrel, and leaned the weapon gently in a far corner.

"Don't look," he told the children, who had not moved since pulling the covers over their heads. Felipe took a blanket from the window and threw it over his father, then dragged the body back into the darkness from where it had first appeared.

"Bueno, mijos, we must go now," said Felipe. "Put on your shoes. Take your covers. Wrap them around you."

While the children tucked blankets around themselves, Felipe wrestled the chiffonier away from its post, then returned to the darkness to get a clean blouse for his mother. They hadn't thought of that. He pulled the one nearest his grasp from his mother's closet, then returned to her side and coaxed his mother to her feet. He helped her unbutton the contaminated shirt, turning her front side away from himself while he wrested her arms from the sleeves. Assisting Maggie with the clean blouse, Felipe averted his eyes, concentrating only on the closures, when he turned her toward himself to button her back up again.

"Dispénsame, Señora," said Felipe.

"Sí, mijo, está bien."

Retrieving his mother's coat, Felipe guided his mother's arms through the sleeves and fastened the front.

"Put on your coat, Mama. Come with me."

He used a dish towel to wipe blood from her face and pull pellets of flesh from her hair. The children lined up at the door, facing forward like little monks in differently colored vestments, and waited silently until Felipe came to the head of the procession. The next oldest child fell to the back of the line to make sure the younger children kept up. Maggie walked next to Felipe, holding on to his hand. Felipe led the family out of the room, out of the house, down the dirt road, faintly lit by a million stars set in a clear winter sky, knowing exactly where they were all going.

Sheriff Max went to his front door knowing there was trouble on the other side of it. The only good news that can come in the middle of the night is a child being born, and tonight the Venezuela family wasn't expecting any such news.

Max looked through the peephole to find Maggie Serna and her oldest boy standing on his porch steps with a half dozen kids in tow; it didn't require all twenty years of his experience as a sheriff to know he wasn't going to like what they had to say. Through the door he told Maggie to wait a moment until he got his wife, then he went back to the bedroom and asked Perlita to answer the door while he dressed. Sheriff Max was not the sort of man who exchanged conversation with anyone except Perlita while in any state of undress. He was a proper man, governed by protocol and the religion he'd learned at his mother's knee. He spoke melodic Spanish and perfect English. His style was to blink twice behind his steel-rimmed glasses and size up a situation better than the people who were in it. No one argued with Maximillan Venezuela. If he told a crowd to disperse, it dispersed. If he told the terror of the El Nido Bar, Napoleón Zapato, to go home because he'd had enough, Napoleón went home. Not only because Max was a huge man himself, but because everyone who knew him believed he was a Spanish Solomon who had only their best interests at heart. He used few words to adjudicate common sense. His hands were like baseball mitts and his head sat upon his shoulders without a neck to interrupt the appearance of a human brick wall. When he walked into a bar, men quit cussing and lonely women pretended they had come only to look for a friend. And Max was sure that was true. He believed that everyone sitting in a bar was there looking for a friend and his heart went out to them. Not enough to let them get away with anything, but enough that he was not a cruel man. He treated people who got crossways with his path rather like children who needed understanding but firm discipline. He never raised his voice or said anything twice. The people of El Nido both feared him and respected his every proclamation.

Perla answered the door dressed in a chenille robe covering a flannel gown, her waist-length graying hair tied back with a silver hair clutch. She put her hands out to Maggie and in a low, sympathetic command, said, "Come in, come in. You must be so cold."

Perla settled the Serna family in her living room and in less than a minute Sheriff Max came out of the bedroom fully dressed. He wasted no time asking Maggie how he might be of help.

What he heard made him nervous. He wasn't sure who had killed Jorge since both Maggie and her son were claiming to have pulled the trigger. Maggie wasn't exactly "claiming"; it was more as if she was chanting, "I killed Jorge. I killed Jorge."

Perla decided it was a good time to hustle Maggie's children into the kitchen for a glass of warm milk. The scene was an eerie one. Instead of clambering and chattering and shoving each other into the kitchen, these children walked slowly, silently into Perla's kitchen and lined the far wall while they watched her pull mugs from a cupboard and wrestle a gallon jug of milk from the refrigerator.

In the living room Felipe was determined to give a full confession, but every time he tried to commence, Maggie droned, "I killed Jorge." Sheriff Max figured that if she looked the same when it came time for court as she did that night, she'd get off on an insanity plea without a hitch. In the meantime, he wasn't sure whom to arrest or what to do with the rest of the family bundled in blankets and lining the wall of his kitchen, once he did.

Max didn't like child beaters, so he'd never had much use for Jorge. He didn't much like wife beaters, either, but his culture had taught him that domestic violence was part of some people's domestic bliss—Dolores and Geraldo Álvarez came to mind—and he allowed himself to sleep at night by thinking that a grown woman could do something about it if she really wanted to. Max had not heard of "battered wife syndrome"; indeed, at that time, neither had the world.

Max's wife was the one who finally made the decision. She scattered the children around the floor, handing them her best floral sofa pillows, put Maggie to bed in the extra room after making her drink a demitasse of whiskey, and told Max he could arrest anybody he wanted to in the morning. Perlita took her husband by the hand and led him into their bedroom, where the light stayed on for another hour.

Only Felipe lay restlessly awake throughout the night. He heard the voices of Sheriff Max and Perlita, but couldn't make out what they were saying, then heard nothing as minutes ticked away. Sometime later the silhouettes of Max and Perlita crept past the sleeping children and the engine of a car started up.

Felipe had no way of knowing that the start of the car also meant the beginning of a lie that would endure for the rest of his life and the lives of everyone there that night.

The next morning, Maggie came out of her whiskey sleep throwing her hands up as if to fend off an attack. Instead of facing someone who meant her harm, she looked into the faces of Perla and Max. She saw her son slip into the room and stand just behind them.

"Maggie," said Max, "we're going to take you and the kids home now."

Maggie's eyes widened and Perla rushed to take hold of her hand and sit with their shoulders leaned into each other. "The body is gone, Maggie," said Perla. "It's been taken to the Gonzales Mortuary. Arrangements have been made. Now you must listen very carefully to what Max has to say."

Max moved one of his huge hands over his jaw, then hung his thumbs in his belt. He looked at Felipe and motioned for him to sit on the other side of his mother.

"When Jorge came home last night, he was very drunk. He meant to harm you, Maggie, you and the kids. That's why he had the gun."

"But he didn't . . ." began Maggie. She wondered if Max had heard a word that had been said the night before.

"Yes he did, Maggie. He had the gun and meant to harm you. But he was so drunk that after he loaded it, he stumbled and the gun went off. Do you understand, Maggie? Jorge fell on his own gun and killed himself."

Sheriff Max wanted to command Maggie to "Repeat after me," but he didn't. This was either going to work or it wouldn't. In Max's mind, if it worked, it meant he had done the right thing and would be able to forgive himself for the misuse of his power. If it didn't—he refused to think about what would happen if it didn't.

"I'm going to type up a statement for you, Maggie, and you're going to sign it. You too, Felipe. The statement will get turned in with my report."

"Won't they know? Won't they be able to tell?" asked Felipe.

"It's all been taken care of, hijo," said Sheriff Max. Then, with a derisive chuckle meant for himself, Max added, "As long as they don't look too close."

Maggie was shaking her head. "I can't let you do this."

Max smiled at Maggie and said, "Señora, if you hadn't said that, I would have been very disappointed in you. But you must think of your son."

"But *I* killed . . ."

"Maggie," Max said after taking a deep breath, "your son is not going to let you say that all on your own. You'll be taking the blame for Jorge and your son will be right there beside you saying *he* was the one who did it." Max looked at his wife, then down at the floor. "Maggie, if they have you, they'll have Felipe. And those kids out there won't have anybody."

It looked as if nothing had happened in the room—except it was cleaner than Maggie had seen it in years. The chiffonier and sofa were back in their places; the children's cocoa mugs had been cleared and washed and sat drying on a clean dishcloth. There were no spatters on the walls.

The blankets had been pulled from the curtain rods and a fire smoldered in the wood stove. The house seemed warm, inviting—

but it only would have looked that way to strangers. To the Serna family it felt like being surrounded by a nightmare—and after the family went back into their home, the torture continued.

If the wind blew a shutter, it reminded them of pounding fists. Reflections in the windows during a storm became dark, roaring apparitions. The crackle of an otherwise soothing fire sometimes sounded like footsteps creaking on decayed porch boards. The place where Jorge's body had lain under a blanket for half a night was treated like an abyss, everyone walking in circles around the spot as if it might open up and swallow them whole.

It was Felipe who sat his mother down at the kitchen table and made her understand that the family was living as if Jorge was still there—because in a way he was. Felipe pointed out that the children were still tiptoeing quietly around the house because the ghost of Jorge was in every board, every nail, in every brick of adobe in the house. Maggie knew this was true, but the idea of moving was difficult for her. The first drop of blood coursing through her veins was created in El Nido. She had lived her whole life there, and her whole soul was made of the generations who had come before her. But she also knew that Felipe was right and she finally acquiesced when he said Albuquerque would be a good place since there were plenty of jobs and a small cluster of family that would be happy to reunite with Maggie and her brood.

Perla collected rent from the little house the Sernas left behind and sent it to Maggie every month. The rent was paid by Hilario Armenta, a man who moved in with ghosts of his own, so there was no room for Jorge. Slamming doors in a storm reminded him of a childhood filled with brothers and sisters, all coming and going through his mother's kitchen. Creaking boards were simply the sounds of a home being used. Nothing more.

Sheriff Max resumed ruling his domain with an iron fist covered by kid leather. He slept well at night and took care of his town during the day, spending the rest of his life comfortable with the decision he'd made, believing that not all crimes are sins, and not all mandates are steeped in morality.

On her deathbed some thirty years later, Maggie told the truth of her husband's murder to a priest and begged God to forgive her.

Felipe never asked forgiveness from anyone his whole life.

Holding Woman

Holding Woman sat on the bench in front of Farmer's Market. It was common for her to be in the very spot where she now sat during these same hours on most Mondays and Wednesdays—and Saturdays for sure. Saturdays were the most important days to be in front of the market. They were the busiest. That was when people needed her the most.

But this was a Monday and most people had done their heavy shopping over the weekend. The customers entering and exiting the market on Mondays were in a hurry. They were lone shoppers picking up what had been forgotten, gathering a short list of things they juggled in their arms while standing in the line marked 15 ITEMS OR LESS. They acknowledged Holding Woman with a wave, the tip of a hat, or an audible hello and a quick smile. These greetings she returned with a nod of her head.

She waited. Someone would stop soon.

Holding Woman's real name was Emily Trujillo, but after the fire, that terrible fire in which all was lost, people seldom used her given name. She still answered to her birth name when it was called, but mainly in the way an animal answers to a command: it sounded familiar and she knew she was supposed to respond to it, but Holding Woman no longer thought of herself as being anyone in particular.

When she was still Emily, Holding Woman raised chickens, selling the extra eggs to neighbor women she'd known all her life.

On Saturdays it was her habit to rise before dawn, gather a dozen eggs, and deliver a basket. Her "egg route," she called it. It brought in very little money, barely over what it took to buy more chicken feed, but money had nothing to do with Emily's egg route. Each Saturday morning she left her sleeping husband and almost-grown daughters and arrived just before six o'clock at the home of someone she liked very much. They drank strong cowboy coffee while buttering slabs of homemade bread or round tortillas, and interrupted each other while talking with their mouths full.

The day of the fire, Emily was visiting the home of Hortencia Alcón, a strong-willed woman who would later arrange her own death. Hortencia did not believe in clinging to life once a person became a decaying bother to those around her, and she said as much to Emily that morning as they sat drinking their coffee. Emily responded that there wasn't much to be done about God's timing or heaven's choice concerning a person's manner of death, so if Hortencia's fate was to lie in bed taking some amount of time being a bother to others until she died, then that's just the way it was going to be.

Hortencia felt no compulsion to debate something she'd already decided, so she simply tilted her head to let Emily know her point had been heard. Years later, when God's choice of disease became known to Hortencia, she walked out into the rangeland of Pump Canyon and sat against a snow-covered rock. She had heard that once the shivering stopped, freezing to death was like going to sleep. Hortencia believed herself capable of enduring a little shivering in order to die the way she wanted. She abhorred news reports of suicide by gun, the mess it left for others to clean up, the guilt it left for others to endure. She felt that freezing to death was a thoughtful method of committing suicide. There would be no mess, no legacy of guilt, and if found before spring, her body would carry no stench. Although Hortencia had never been disoriented a day in her life, everyone would think she had become a doddering old woman who had wandered off and sat too long resting herself. She knew she wouldn't be fooling God—she would deal with him later; she meant only to fool those she left behind.

Thinking of how she was not going to endure a long illness, how she was going to fool everyone, and that the priest at Our Lady of the Blessed Virgen de Guadalupe was the one she most wanted to fool, prompted Hortencia to begin talking about Father Morris. In spite of herself, Emily chortled when Hortencia said, "The old goat is too cheap to turn on the heat in the church. Pero he can afford un dish de satélite, ¿verdad? Y la señora Lobato says he buys cerveza todos los viernes. Sí. Una case de Budweiser, every Friday." Hortencia tore off another piece of tortilla and waved it in Emily's direction before popping it into her mouth. "They should call it 'Bud-stupider' if you ask me."

Emily felt that Hortencia's complaints were quite blasphemous, but she couldn't help laughing at the truth when Hortencia described Sunday Mass—everyone bundled inside of coats, their breath rolling out of their mouths like puffs of fog when it came time for the congregation to join in the liturgy.

Hortencia venomously wondered about a priest who professed unwavering love for his "children" and then made it uncomfortable for his parishioners to come to church.

That was all Emily had meant to do when she built the fire in the wood-burning stove, just as she had done for years and years. She did not want her family getting up and seeing their breath. She didn't want them to be cold or suffer any sort of discomfort.

She didn't know that the chimney had developed a crack, and through that crack little sparks of fire were flying against the beams inside the wall. All Emily knew when she got back to her house was that the El Nido volunteer fire department had made it to her home before she did and there were four bodies lying inside the home where she had left a fire burning.

W hen she was still Emily, she was married to a man who gave her three daughters. Emily and her husband had married at sixteen and the union became one of those miracles of commitment. They agreed on how to spend their money, they followed their religion, they held the same things as important, and they cooperated in all the ways it takes to make a secure home for happy children.

Every night when they tucked their daughters into bed, they told them a lovely story, a wise fable, or a mythological tale, taking a long time to get to the end. Emily and her husband wanted their girls to fall into the deepest of sleeps, then dream of Pegasus carrying them to a land far from the grasp of meanness and disappointment. Emily told them the story "The Lamb With the Golden Fleece," which taught them that the pain of life is relieved with laughter. Her husband recited the story "The Three Caskets," about the woman who chose God over gold and then received more riches than she'd ever imagined.

Emily and her husband gave these stories to their daughters to take away the world in which they lived and replace it with a world where things are fair, wise, and gentle, and everything makes sense—if only for a few minutes.

F rom among the debris of the fire, Emily gathered the things left behind by her family, holding them close to her heart and up against her cheek. Holding these things close to her face, she felt sure they still held the smell of her daughters' clean nightgowns and body soap. She found the hairbrush of one of her daughters and used it on her own hair, then pulled the commingled strands away from the bristles and saved them in a silk pouch.

The mourners thought Emily had great strength because she sat through the funeral without expression. But they were wrong. At this funeral Emily did not sit quietly out of strength; she sat quietly because she had become someone else and was as yet unfamiliar with who that person was to be. She no longer recognized herself, and the world would never make sense to her again, except in stories.

A t first, the nurses at San Joaquin hospital thought the woman who came in asking to hold babies had lost her mind. They were right, of course, and yet the eyes that implored them hadn't looked crazed. It was Salina Gonzales who remembered an article from a medical journal talking about how hospitals in big cities used volunteers to hold babies born and abandoned by drug-addicted mothers. It said the babies often died from "failure to thrive." It took someone else holding them to keep them alive. Someone else had to will them to live because they too suffered from the same illness of despair that was killing their mothers.

The hospitals used volunteers because the nurses were too busy and there weren't enough of them to sit for hours holding babies. As with every hospital, the nurses at San Joaquin had babies born to alcoholic mothers, now confined to the detox center since giving birth. Salina gave Emily a sterilized gown and mask and sat her down in a rocking chair. Settling a baby into her arms, Salina told Emily that she could stay for three hours each day and there was no pay.

Every day Holding Woman came to the hospital and held the scrawniest, most helpless of human beings. She told them the same stories she had told her daughters. She told them of Artemis, the goddess of all wild nature, who dances in forests accompanied by nymphs. She told them of Hercules and his twelve impossible tasks and whispered that all humans must attempt impossible tasks; the first task for the babies was to live. She said, "Did you know that Hercules fought his first battle as a baby? Jealous Hera sent two snakes to his crib, but in her rage she had underestimated his strength. Hercules grabbed the serpents by the throat and squeezed the monsters with his baby fists until they fell lifeless at his feet."

She told the babies that they, too, now battled a serpent and they must fight like Hercules. She told them that the gods had sent them to the mortal world to teach true bravery to others.

The babies lay on Holding Woman's chest and slept, sighed, and breathed—and eventually lived. If there were no babies fighting for their lives, she held the healthy ones, or walked into rooms where dying people lay in delirious slumber. It didn't matter to Holding Woman if they were unaware that she held a hand or patted a forehead. It didn't matter that they were grown-ups; she told them the same stories. She reminded the dying people of the wealth they had accumulated.

"The gods of New Mexico gave you snow the color of blue diamonds when the moon shines full, and hand-painted sunsets, every evening a different canvas. The night sky was your oracle, freely confiding your destiny. Your children and those who love you are your wealth. There are no pockets in shrouds," Holding Woman said, "but all of this you are allowed to take with you."

One day Holding Woman left the hospital and stopped at Farmer's Market to buy some simple groceries. She was very tired that day, so she had to rest herself on the outside bench before going in. It was there that she became Holding Woman to the world outside the hospital.

Maggie Serna, looking troubled and exhausted, was on her way into the store carrying her youngest child. The child wanted to do grocery shopping even less than her mother, so she whined and struggled against her mother's clutch. Seeing this, Holding Woman put out her arms and said, "Let me have the child. I will tell her a story while you do your marketing." When Maggie wheeled her cart out of the store, there sat the woman she'd always known as Emily Trujillo with the child snuggled against her bosom and listening to how rainbows are really cherubs writing promises in the sky with colored pencils in a secret language that only children know how to read.

Now Holding Woman not only held babies and dying people at the hospital, she held the children of overworked mothers, and sometimes held the mothers themselves. It became so common to see someone leaning into Holding Woman's chest outside Farmer's Market and listening to stories, that no one paid much attention—unless of course it was someone who wished she had gotten there first. Grown women stopped when they saw Emily on the bench and asked, "Holding Woman, can I have a hug too?"

Holding Woman always gathered them inside a warm arm and began to tell them a story or a parable or how the gods made weather. If it was spring, she told them of Persephone emerging from the darkness. If there was to be an eclipse, she said Pegasus was flying too near the sun and his great wings blocked the light. She said the flamingo sunsets of summer were the warm glow of ovens used by angels to bake cookies for children living in heaven.

She told Jimmy De La Cruz Aesop's fable "The Trumpeter Taken Prisoner," reciting from memory the last line: "He who incites others to war is worse than he who fights." She told him that it requires more courage to resist what is wrong than it does to assist in the destruction of what is right, and that there are indeed times that the bravest action a person can take is to surrender.

She held Betty and described the bottomless abyss of forgiveness that small children hold in their hearts for their parents. She told Betty to go home and allow her children to love her.

Beany Moreno asked Holding Woman if God made allowance for extenuating circumstances when deciding his punishment for sins. Holding Woman assured her that the universe understands all actions and circumstances.

She reminded Adolfo to treasure true friendship of any duration, and not allow grief for the present to muddle sweet memories of the past. "Grieve," said Holding Woman, "but do not despair."

At the end of the stories, Holding Woman said to each of them that it's all right to be grown up and still need holding and to be told stories. Holding Woman said grown-ups are really just children who have forgotten their fairy tales.